A T

PENGUIN BOOKS
A THEFT

Saul Bellow was awarded the Nobel Prize for Literature in 1976. His novel, *Humboldt's Gift,* won the Pulitzer Prize the previous year. He is the only novelist to receive three National Book Awards, for *The Adventures of Augie March; Herzog;* and *Mr. Sammler's Planet. A Theft* is his fourteenth book.

A THEFT

Saul·Bellow

PENGUIN BOOKS
Published by the Penguin Group
Viking Penguin Inc., 40 West 23rd Street,
New York, New York 10010, U.S.A.
Penguin Books Ltd, 27 Wrights Lane,
London W8 5TZ, England
Penguin Books Australia Ltd, Ringwood,
Victoria, Australia
Penguin Books Canada Ltd, 2801 John Street,
Markham, Ontario, Canada L3R 1B4
Penguin Books (N.Z.) Ltd, 182-190 Wairau Road,
Auckland 10, New Zealand

Penguin Books Ltd, Registered Offices:
Harmondsworth, Middlesex, England

First published in Penguin Books 1989
Published simultaneously in Canada

1 3 5 7 9 10 8 6 4 2

LIBRARY OF CONGRESS CATALOGING IN PUBLICATION DATA

Bellow, Saul.
A theft : a novella / by Saul Bellow.
p.   cm.
ISBN 0–14–011969–8
I. Title.
PS3503.E4488T4 1989
813′.52—dc19   88–29261

Printed in the United States of America
Set in Bodoni
Designed by Michael Ian Kaye

To my son, Daniel O. Bellow

A THEFT

Clara Velde, to begin with what was conspicuous about her, had short blond hair, fashionably cut, growing upon a head unusually big. In a person of an inert character a head of such size might have seemed a deformity; in Clara, because she had so much personal force, it came across as ruggedly handsome. She needed that head; a mind like hers demanded space. She was big-boned; her shoulders were not broad but high. Her blue eyes, exceptionally large, grew prominent when she brooded. The nose was small—ancestrally a North Sea nose. The mouth was very good but stretched extremely wide when she grinned, when she wept. Her forehead was powerful. When she came to the threshold of middle age, the lines of her naive charm deepened; they would be permanent now. Really, everything about her was conspicuous, not only the size and shape of her head. She must have decided long ago that for the likes of her there could be no cover-up; she couldn't divert energy into disguises. So there she was, a rawboned American woman. She had very good legs—who knows what you would have seen if pioneer women had worn shorter skirts. She bought her clothes in the best shops and was knowledgeable about cosmetics. Nevertheless the backcountry look never left her. She came from the sticks; there could be no mistake about that. Her people? Indiana and Illinois farmers and small-town businessmen who were very religious. Clara was brought up on the Bible: prayers at breakfast, grace at every meal, psalms learned by heart, the Gospels, chapter and verse—old-time religion. Her father owned small department stores in southern Indiana. The children were sent to good schools. Clara had studied Greek at Bloomington and Elizabethan-Jacobean literature at Wellesley. A disappointing love affair in Cambridge led to a suicide attempt. The family decided not to bring her back to Indiana. When she threatened to swallow more sleeping pills they allowed her to attend Columbia University, and she lived in New York under close supervision—the regimen organized by her parents. She, however, found ways to do exactly as she pleased. She feared hellfire but she did it just the same.

After a year at Columbia she went to work at Reuters, then she taught in a private school and later wrote American feature articles for British and Australian papers. By the age of forty she had formed a company of her own—a journalistic agency specializing in high fashion for women—and eventually she sold this company to an international publishing group and became one of its executives. In the boardroom she was referred to by some as "a good corporate person," by others as "the czarina of fashion writing." By now she was also the attentive mother of three small girls. The first of these was conceived with some difficulty (the professional assistance of gynecologists made it possible). The father of these children was Clara's fourth husband.

Three of the four had been no more than that—men who fell into the husband class. Only one, the third, had been something like the real thing. That was Spontini the oil tycoon, a close friend of the billionaire leftist and terrorist Giangiacomo F., who blew himself up in the seventies. (Some Italians said, predictably, that the government had set him up to explode.) Mike Spontini was not political, but then he wasn't born rich, like Giangiacomo, whose role model had been Fidel Castro. Spontini made his own fortune. His looks, his town houses and châteaus and yachts, would have qualified him for a role in *La Dolce Vita*. Scores of women were in pursuit. Clara had won the fight to marry him but lost the fight to keep him. Recognizing at last that he was getting rid of her, she didn't oppose this difficult, arbitrary man and surrendered all property rights in the settlement—a nonsettlement really. He took away the terrific gifts he had made her, down to the last bracelet. No sooner had the divorce come through than Mike was bombed out by two strokes. He was half paralyzed now and couldn't form his words. An Italian Sairey Gamp type took care of him in Venice, where Clara occasionally went to see him. Her ex-husband would give her an animal growl, one glare of rage, and then resume his look of imbecility. He would rather be an imbecile on the Grand Canal than a husband on Fifth Avenue.

The other husbands—one married in a full-dress church wedding, the others routine city hall jobs—were . . . well, to be plain about it, gesture-husbands. Velde was big and handsome, indolent, defiantly incompetent. He worked on the average no longer than six months at any job. By then everybody in the organization wanted to kill him.

His excuse for being in and out of work was that his

true talent was for campaign strategies. Elections brought out the best in him: getting media attention for his candidate, who never, ever, won in the primaries. But then, he disliked being away from home, and an election is a traveling show. "Very sweet," went one of Clara's summaries to Laura Wong, the Chinese-American dress designer who was her confidante. "An affectionate father as long as the kids don't bother him, what Wilder mostly does is sit reading paperbacks—thrillers, science fiction and pop biographies. I think he feels that all will be well as long as he keeps sitting there on his cushions. To him inertia is the same as stability. Meantime I run the house single-handed: mortgage, maintenance, housemaids, au pair girls from France or Scandinavia—Austrian the latest. I dream up projects for the children, I do the school bit, do the dentist and the pediatrician, plus playmates, outings, psychological tests, doll dressing, cutting and pasting valentines. What else . . . ? Work with their secret worries, sort out their quarrels, encourage their minds, wipe tears. Love them. Wilder just goes on reading P. D. James, or whoever, till I'm ready to snatch the book and throw it in the street."

One Sunday afternoon she did exactly that—opened the window first and skimmed his paperback into Park Avenue.

"Was he astonished?" asked Ms. Wong.

"Not absolutely. He sees how provoking he is. What he doesn't allow is that I have reason to be provoked. He's *there*, isn't he? What else do I want? In all the turbulence, he's the point of calm. And for all the wild times and miseries I had in the love game—about which he has full information—he's the answer. A sexy woman who couldn't find the place to put her emotionality, and appealing to brilliant men who couldn't do what she really wanted done."

"And he *does* do?"

"He's the overweening overlord, and for no other reason than sexual performance. It's stud power that makes him so confident. He's not the type to think it out. *I* have to do that. A sexy woman may delude herself about the gratification of a mental life. But what really settles everything, according to him, is masculine bulk. As close as he comes to spelling it out, his view is that I wasted time on Jaguar nonstarters. Lucky for me I came across a genuine Rolls-Royce. But he's got the wrong car," she said, crossing the kitchen with efficient haste to take the kettle off the boil. Her stride was powerful, her awkward, shapely legs going too quickly for the heels to keep pace. "Maybe a Lincoln Continental would be more like it. Anyway, no woman wants her bedroom to be a garage, and least of all for a boring car."

What was a civilized lady like Laura Wong making of such confidences? The raised Chinese cheek with the Chinese eye let into it, the tiny degree of heaviness of the epicanthic fold all the whiter over the black of the eye, and the light of that eye, so foreign to see and at the same time superfamiliar in its sense . . . What could be more human than the recognition of this familiar sense?

And yet Laura Wong was very much a New York lady in her general understanding of things. She did not confide in Clara as fully as Clara confided in her. But then who did, who *could* make a clean breast so totally? What Ms. Wong's rich eyes suggested, Clara in her awkwardness tried in fact to say. To do.

"Yes, the books," said Laura. "You can't miss that." She had also seen Wilder Velde pedaling his Exercycle while the TV ran at full volume.

"He can't understand what's wrong, since what I make looks like enough for us. But I don't earn *all* that much, with three kids in private schools. So family money has to be spent. That involves my old parents—sweet old Bible Hoosiers. I can't make him see that I can't afford an unemployed husband, and there isn't a headhunter in New York who'll talk to Wilder after one look at his curriculum vitae and his job record. Three months here, five months there. Because it's upsetting me, and for *my* sake, my bosses are trying to place him somewhere. I'm important enough to the corporation for that. If he loves elections so much, maybe he should run for office. He *looks* congressional, and what do I care if he screws up in the House of Representatives. I've been with congressmen, I even married one, and he's no dumber than they are. But he won't admit that anything is wrong; he's got that kind of confidence in himself—so much that he can even take a friendly interest in the men I've been involved with. They're like failed competitors to the guy who won the silver trophy. He's proud to claim a connection with the famous ones, and when I went to visit poor Mike in Venice, he flew with me."

"So he isn't jealous," said Laura Wong.

"The opposite. The people I've been intimate with, to him are like the folks in a history book. And suppose Richard III or Metternich had gotten into *your* wife's pants when she was a girl? Wilder is a name-dropper, and the names he most enjoys dropping are the ones he came into by becoming my husband. Especially the head-liners . . ."

Laura Wong was of course aware that it was not for her to mention the most significant name of all, the name that haunted all of Clara's confidences. That was for Clara herself to bring up. Whether it was appropriate, whether she could summon the strength to deal with the most persistent of her preoccupations, whether she would call on Laura to bear with her one more time . . . these were choices you had to trust her to make tactfully.

". . . whom he sometimes tapes when they're being interviewed on CBS or the MacNeil/Lehrer programs. Teddy Regler always the foremost."

Yes, there was the name. Mike Spontini mattered greatly, but you had to see him still in the husband category. Ithiel Regler stood much higher with Clara than any of the husbands. "On a scale of ten," she liked to say to Laura, "he *was* ten."

"Is ten?" Laura had suggested.

"I'd not only be irrational but psycho to keep Teddy

in the active present tense," Clara had said. This was a clouded denial. Wilder Velde continued to be judged by a standard from which Ithiel Regler could never be removed. It did not make, it never could make, good sense to speak of irrationality and recklessness. Clara never would be safe or prudent, and she wouldn't have dreamed of expelling Ithiel's influence—not even if God's angel had offered her the option. She might have answered: You might as well try to replace my own sense of touch with somebody else's. And the matter would have had to stop there.

So Velde, by taping Ithiel's programs for her, proved how unassailable he was in his position as the final husband, the one who couldn't in the scheme of things be bettered. "And I'm glad the man thinks that," said Clara. "It's best for all of us. He wouldn't believe that I might be unfaithful. You've got to admire *that*. So here's a double-mystery couple. Which is the more mysterious one? Wilder actually enjoys watching Ithiel being so expert and smart from Washington. And meantime, Laura, I have no sinful ideas of being unfaithful. I don't even think about such things, they don't figure in my conscious mind. Wilder and I have a sex life no marriage counselor in the world could fault. We have three children, and I'm a loving mother, I bring them up conscientiously. But when Ithiel comes to town and I see him at lunch, I start to flow for him. He used to make me come by stroking my cheek. It can happen when he talks to me. Or even when I see him on TV or just hear his voice. *He* doesn't know it—I think not—and anyway Ithiel wouldn't want to do harm, interfere, dominate or exploit—that's not the way he is. We have this total, delicious connection, which is also a disaster. But even to a woman raised on the Bible, which in the city of New York in this day and age is a pretty remote influence, you couldn't call my attachment an evil that rates punishment after death. It's not the sex offenses that will trip you up, because by now nobody can draw the line between natural and unnatural in sex. Anyway, it couldn't be a woman's hysteria that would send her to hell. It would be something else. . . ."

"What else?" Laura asked. But Clara was silent, and Laura wondered whether it wasn't Teddy Regler who should be asked what Clara considered a mortal sin. He had known Clara so well, over so many years, that perhaps he could explain what she meant.

This Austrian au pair girl, Miss Wegman—Clara gave herself the pleasure of sizing her up. She checked off the points: dressed appropriately for an interview, hair freshly washed, no long nails, no conspicuous polish. Clara herself was gotten up as a tailored matron, in a tortoise-shell-motif suit and a white blouse with a ruff under the chin. From her teaching days she commanded a task-mistress's way of putting questions ("Now, Willie, pick up the *Catiline* and give me the tense of *abutere* in Cicero's opening sentence"): it was the disciplinarian's armor worn by a softy. This Austrian chick made a pleasing impression. The father was a Viennese bank official and the kid was correct, civil and sweet. You had to put it out of your head that Vienna was a hatchery of psychopaths and Hitlerites. Think instead of that dear beauty in the double suicide with the crown prince. This child, who had an Italian mother, was called Gina. She spoke English fluently and probably wasn't faking when she said she could assume responsibility for three little girls. Not laying secret plans to con everybody, not actually full of dislike for defiant, obstinate, mutely resistant kids like Clara's eldest, Lucy, a stout little girl needing help. A secretly vicious young woman could do terrible damage to a kid like Lucy, give her wounds that would never heal. The two little skinny girls laughed at their sister. They scooped up their snickers in their hands while Lucy held herself like a Roman soldier. Her face was heated with boredom and grievances.

The foreign young lady made all the right moves, came up with the correct answers—why not? since the questions made them obvious. Clara realized how remote from present-day "facts of life" and current history her "responsible" assumptions were—those were based on her small-town Republican churchgoing upbringing, the nickel-and-dime discipline of her mother, who clicked out your allowance from the bus conductor's changemaker hanging from her neck. Life in that Indiana town was already as out of date as ancient Egypt. The "decent people" there were the natives from whom television evangelists raised big money to pay for their stretch limos and Miami-style vices. Those were Clara's preposterous dear folks, by whom she had felt stifled in childhood and for whom she now felt a boundless love. In Lucy she saw her own people, rawboned, stubborn, silent—she saw herself. Much could be made of such beginnings. But how did you coach a kid like this, what could you do for her in New York City?

"Now—is it all right to call you Gina?—what was your purpose, Gina, in coming to New York?"

"To perfect my English. I'm registered in a music course at Columbia. And to learn about the U.S.A."

A well-brought-up and vulnerable European girl would have done better to go to Bemidji, Minnesota. Any idea of the explosive dangers girls faced here? They could be blown up from within. When she was young (and not only then), Clara had made reckless experiments—all those chancy relationships; anything might have happened; much did; and all for the honor of running risks. This led her to resurvey Miss Wegman, to estimate what might be done to a face like hers, its hair, her figure, the bust—to the Arabian Nights treasure that nubile girls (innocent up to a point) were sitting on. So many dangerous attractions—and such ignorance! Naturally Clara felt that she herself would do everything (up to a point) to protect a young woman in her household, and everything possible meant using all the resources of an experienced person. At the same time it was a fixed belief with Clara that no *in*experienced woman of mature years could be taken seriously. So could it be a serious Mrs. Wegman back in Vienna, the mother, who had given this Gina permission to spend a year in Gogmagogsville? In the alternative, a rebellious Gina was chancing it on her own. Again, for the honor of running risks.

Clara, playing matron, lady of the house, nodded to agree with her own thoughts, and this nod may have been interpreted by the girl to mean that it was okay, she was as good as hired. She'd have her own decent room in this vast Park Avenue co-op apartment, a fair wage, house privileges, two free evenings, two afternoons for the music-history classes, parts of the morning while the children were at school. Austrian acquaintances, eligible young people, were encouraged to visit, and American friends vetted by Clara. By special arrangement, Gina could even give a small party. You can be democratic and still have discipline.

The first months, Clara watched her new au pair girl closely, and then she was able to tell friends at lunch, people in the office, and even her psychiatrist, Dr. Gladstone, how lucky she had been to find this Viennese Miss Wegman with darling manners. What a desirable role model she was, and also such a calming influence on the hyperexcitable tots. "As you have said, Doctor, they set off hysterical tendencies in one another."

You didn't expect replies from these doctors. You paid them to lend you their ears. Clara said as much to Ithiel Regler, with whom she remained very much in touch— frequent phone calls, occasional letters, and when Ithiel came up from Washington they had drinks, even dinner from time to time.

"If you think this Gladstone is really helping . . . I suppose some of those guys *can* be okay," said Ithiel, neutral in tone. With him there was no trivial meddling. He never tried to tell you what to do, never advised on family matters.

"It's mostly to relieve my heart," said Clara. "If you and I had become husband and wife that wouldn't have been necessary. I might not be so overcharged. But even so, we have open lines of communication to this day. In fact, you went through a shrink period yourself."

"I sure did. But my doctor had even more frailties than me."

"Does that matter?"

"I guess not. But it occurred to me one day that he couldn't tell me how to be Teddy Regler. And nothing would go well unless I *was* Teddy Regler. Not that I make cosmic claims for precious Teddy, but there never was anybody else for me to be."

Because he thought things out he spoke confidently, and because of his confidence he sounded full of himself. But there was less conceit about Ithiel than people imputed to him. In company, Clara, speaking as one who knew, really *knew* him—and she made no secret of that— would say, when his name was mentioned, when he was put down by some restless spirit or other, that Ithiel Regler was more plainspoken about his own faults than anybody who felt it necessary to show him up.

At this turn in their psychiatry conversation, Clara made a move utterly familiar to Ithiel. Seated, she inclined her upper body toward him. "*Tell* me!" she said. When she did that, he once more saw the country girl in all the dryness of her ignorance, appealing for instruction. Her mouth would be slightly open as he made his answer. She would watch and listen with critical concentration. "Tell!" was one of her code words.

Ithiel said, "The other night I watched a child-abuse program on TV, and after a while I began to think how much they were putting under that heading short of sexual molestation or *deadly* abuse—mutilation and murder. Most of what they showed was normal punishment in my time. So today I could be a child-abuse case and my father might have been arrested as a child-beater. When he was in a rage he was transformed—he was like moonshine from the hills compared to store-bought booze. The kids, all of us, were slammed two-handed, from both sides simultaneously, and without mercy. So? Forty years later I have to watch a TV show to see that I, too, was abused. Only, I loved my late father. Beating was only an incident, a single item between us. I still love him. Now, to tell you what this signifies: I can't apply the going terms to my case without damage to reality. My father beat me passionately. When he did it, I hated him like poison and murder. I also loved him with a passion, and I'll *never* think myself an abused child. I suspect that your psychiatrist would egg me on to hate, not turn hate into passivity. So he'd be telling me from the height of his theoretical assumptions how Teddy Regler should be Teddy Regler. The real Teddy, however, rejects this grudge against a dead man, whom he more than half expects to see in the land of the dead. If that were to happen, it would be because we loved each other and wished for it. Besides, after the age of forty a moratorium has to be declared—earlier, if possible. You can't afford to be a damaged child forever. That's my argument with psychiatry: it encourages you to build on abuses and keeps you infantile. Now the heart of this whole country aches for itself. There may be occult political causes for this as well. Foreshadowings of the fate of this huge superpower . . ."

Clara said, *"Tell!"* and then she listened like a country girl. That side of her would never go away, thank God, Ithiel thought; while Clara's secret observation was, How well we've come to understand each other. If only we'd been like this twenty years back.

It wasn't as if she hadn't been able to follow him in the early years. She always had understood what Ithiel was saying. If she hadn't he wouldn't have taken the trouble to speak—why waste words? But she also recognized the comic appeal of being the openmouthed rube. Gee! Yeah! Of course! And I could kick myself in the head for not having thought of this myself! But all the while the big-city Clara had been in the making, stockpiling ideas for survival in Gogmagogsville.

"But let me tell you," she said, "what I was too astonished to mention when we were first acquainted

. . . when we lay in bed naked in Chelsea, and you sent thoughts going around the world, but then they always came back to *us*, in bed. In *bed*, which in my mind was for rest, or sex, or reading a novel. And back to *me*, whom you never overlooked, wherever your ideas may have gone."

This Ithiel, completely black-haired then, and now grizzled, had put some weight on. His face had filled, rounded out at the bottom. It had more of an urn shape. Otherwise his looks were remarkably unchanged. He said, "I really didn't have such a lot of good news about the world. I think you were hunting among the obscure things I talked about for openings to lead back to your one and only subject: love and happiness. I often feel as much curiosity about love and happiness now as you did then listening to my brainstorms."

Between jobs, Ithiel had been able to find time to spend long months with Clara—in Washington, his main base, in New York, on Nantucket, and in Montauk. After three years together, she had actually pressured him into buying an engagement ring. She was at that time, as she herself would tell you, terribly driven and demanding (as if she wasn't now). "I needed a symbolic declaration at least," she would say, "and I put such heat on him, saying that he had dragged me around so long as his girl, his lay, that at last I got this capitulation from him." He took Clara to Madison Hamilton's shop in the diamond district and bought her an emerald ring—the real thing, conspicuously clear, color perfect, top of its class, as appraisers later told Clara. Twelve hundred dollars he paid for it, a big price in the sixties, when he was especially strapped. He was like that, though: hard to convince, but once decided, he dismissed the cheaper items. "Take away all this other shit," he muttered. Proper Mr. Hamilton probably had heard this. Madison Hamilton was a gentleman, and reputable and dignified in a decade when some of those qualities were still around: "Before our fellow Americans had lied themselves into a state of hallucination—bullshitted themselves into inanity," said Ithiel. He said also, still speaking of Hamilton, who sold antique jewelry, "I think the weird moniker my parents gave me predisposed me favorably toward vanishing types like Hamilton—Wasps with good manners. . . . For all I know, he might have been an Armenian, passing."

Clara held out her engagement finger, and Ithiel put on the ring. When the check was written and Mr. Hamilton asked for identification, Ithiel was able to show not only a driver's license but a Pentagon pass. It made a great impression. At that time Ithiel was flying high as a wunderkind in nuclear strategy, and he might have gone all the way to the top, to the negotiating table in Geneva, facing the Russians, if he had been less quirky. People of great power set a high value on his smarts. Well, you only had to look at the size and the evenness of his dark eyes—"The eyes of Hera in my Homeric grammar," said Clara. "Except that he was anything but effeminate. No way!" All she meant was that he had a classic level look.

"At Hamilton's that afternoon, I wore a miniskirt suit that showed my knees touching. I haven't got knock-knees, just this minor peculiarity about the inside of my legs. . . . If this is a deformity, it did me good. Ithiel was crazy about it."

At a later time, she mentioned this as "the unforeseen usefulness of anomalies." She wrote that on a piece of paper and let it drift about the house with other pieces of paper, so that if asked what it meant, she could say she had forgotten.

Although Ithiel now and again might mention "game theory" or "MAD," he wouldn't give out information that might be classified, and she didn't even try to understand what he did in Washington. Now and then his name turned up in the *Times* as a consultant on international security, and for a couple of years he was an adviser to the chairman of a Senate committee. She let politics alone, asking no questions. The more hidden his activities, the better she felt about him. Power, danger, secrecy made him even sexier. No loose talk. A woman could feel safe with a man like Ithiel.

It was marvelous luck that the little apartment in Chelsea should be so near Penn Station. When he blew into town he telephoned, and in fifteen minutes he was there, holding his briefcase. It was his habit when he arrived to remove his necktie and stuff it in among his documents. It was her habit when she hung up the phone to take the ring from its locked drawer, admire it on her finger, and kiss it when the doorbell rang.

No, Ithiel didn't make a big public career, he wasn't a team player, he had no talent for administration; he was too special in his thinking, and there was no chance that he would reach cabinet level. Anyway, it was too easy for him to do well as a free agent; he wouldn't latch onto politicians with presidential ambitions: the smart ones never would make it. "And besides," he said, "I like to stay mobile." A change of continent when he wanted fresh air. He took on such assignments as pleased the operator in him, the behind-the-scenes Teddy Regler: in the Persian Gulf, with a Japanese whiskey firm looking for a South American market, with the Italian police tracking terrorists. None of these activities compromised his Washington reputation for dependability. He testified before congressional investigative committees as an expert witness.

In their days of intimacy, Clara more than once helped him to make a deadline. Then they were Teddy and Clara, a superteam working around the clock. He knew how dependable she was, a dervish for work, how quickly she grasped unfamiliar ideas, how tactful she could be. From her side, she was aware how analytically deep he could go, what a range of information he had, how good his reports were. He outclassed everybody, it seemed to her. Once, at the Hotel Cristallo in Cortina d'Ampezzo, they did a document together, to the puncturing rhythm of the tennis court below. He had to read the pages she was typing for him over the transatlantic telephone. While he spoke, he let her run ahead on the machine. He could trust her to organize his notes and write them up in a style resembling his own (not that style mattered in Washington). All but the restricted material. She'd do any amount of labor—long dizzy days at the tinny lightweight Olivetti—to link herself with him.

As she told Ms. Wong, she had seen a book many years ago in the stacks of the Columbia library. A single title had detached itself from the rest, from thousands: *The Human Pair*. Well, the big-boned blond student doing *research* and feeling (unaware) so volcanic that one of her controls was to hold her breath—at the sight of those gilded words on the spine of a book she was able to breathe again. She breathed. She didn't take the book down; she didn't want to read it. "I wanted *not* to read it."

She described this to Laura Wong, who was too polite to limit her, too discreet to direct her confidences into suitable channels. You had to listen to everything that came out of Clara's wild head when she was turned on. Ms. Wong applied these personal revelations to her own experience of life, as anybody else would have done. She had been married too. Five years an American wife. Maybe she had even been in love. She never said. You'd never know.

"The full title was *The Human Pair in the Novels of Thomas Hardy*. At school I loved Hardy, but now all I wanted of that book was the title. It came back to me at Cortina. Ithiel and I were the Human Pair. We took a picnic lunch up to the forest behind the Cristallo—cheese, bread, cold cuts, pickles and wine. I rolled on top of Ithiel and fed him. Later I found out when I tried it myself how hard it is to swallow in that position.

"I now feel, looking back, that I was carrying too much of an electrical charge. It's conceivable that the world-spirit gets into mere girls and makes them its demon interpreters. I mentioned this to Ithiel a while back—he and I are old enough now to discuss such subjects—and he said that one of his Russian dissident pals had been talking to him about something called 'superliterature'—literature being the tragedy or comedy of private lives, while superliterature was about the possible end of the world. Beyond personal history. In Cortina I thought I was acting from personal emotions, but those emotions were so devouring, fervid, that they may have been suprapersonal—a wholesome young woman in love expressing the tragedy or comedy of the world concluding. A fever using love as its carrier.

"After the holiday we drove down to Milan. Actually, that's where I met Spontini. We were at a fancy after-dinner party, and he said, 'Let me give you a ride back to your hotel.' So Ithiel and I got into his Jaguar with him, and we were escorted by carloads of cops, fore and aft. He was proud of his security; this was when the Red Brigades were kidnapping the rich. It wasn't so *easy* to be rich—rich enough for ransom. Mike said, 'For all I know, my own friend Giangiacomo may have a plan to abduct me. Not Giangiacomo personally but the outfit he belongs to.'

"On that same trip Ithiel and I also spent some time with Giangiacomo the billionaire revolutionist himself. He was a kind, pleasant man, good-looking except for his preposterous Fidel Castro getup, like a little kid from Queens in a cowboy suit. He wore a forage cap, and in a corner of his fancy office there was a machine gun on the floor. He invited Ithiel and me to his château, about eighty kilometers away, eighteenth-century rococo: it might have been a set for *The Marriage of Figaro*, except for the swimming pool with algae in it and a sauna alongside, in the dank part of the garden far down the hill. At lunch, the butler was leaning over with truffles from Giangiacomo's own estate to grate over the *crème velou-tée,* and he couldn't because Giangiacomo was waving his arms, going on about revolutionary insurgency, the subject of the book he was writing. Then, when Ithiel told him that there were no views like his in Karl Marx, Giangiacomo said, 'I never read Marx, and it's too late now to do it; it's urgent to act.' He drove us back to Milan in the afternoon at about five hundred miles an hour. Lots of action, let me tell you. I covered my emerald and gripped it with my right hand, to protect it, maybe, in a crash.

"Next day, when we flew out, Giangiacomo was at the airport in battle dress with a group of boutique girls, all in minis. A year or two later he blew himself up while trying to dynamite power lines. I was sad about it."

When they returned to New York in stuffy August,

back to the apartment in Chelsea, Clara cooked Ithiel a
fine Italian dinner of veal with lemon and capers, as good
as, or better than, the Milan restaurants served, or Giangiacomo's chef at the lovely toy château. At work in the
narrow New York galley-style kitchen, Clara was naked
and wore clogs. To make it tender, she banged the meat
with a red cast-iron skillet. In those days she wore her
hair long. Whether she was dressed or nude, her movements always were energetic; she didn't know the meaning of slow-time.

Stretched on the bed, Ithiel studied his dangerous documents (all those forbidden facts) while she cooked and
the music played; the shades were down, the lights were
on, and they enjoyed a wonderful privacy. "When I was
a kid and we went on holidays to the Jersey coast during
the war," Clara recalled, "we had black window blinds
because of the German submarines hiding out there under
the Atlantic, but we could play our radios as loud as we
wanted." She liked to fancy that she was concealing Ithiel
and his secret documents—not that the deadly information affected Ithiel enough to change the expression
of his straight profile: "concentrating like Jascha Heifetz." Could anybody have been tailing him? Guys with
zoom lenses or telescopic sights on the Chelsea rooftops?
Ithiel smiled, and pooh-poohed this. He wasn't that important. "I'm not rich like Spontini." They might rather
be trained on Clara, zeroing in on a Daughter of Albion
without a stitch on, he said.

In those days he came frequently from Washington to visit his young son, who lived with his mother on East Tenth Street. Ithiel's ex-wife, who now used her maiden name, Etta Wolfenstein, went out of her way to be friendly to Clara, chatted her up on the telephone. Etta had informants in Washington, who kept an eye on Ithiel. Ithiel was indifferent to gossip. "I'm not the president," he would say, "that bulletins should go out about my moods and movements."

"I shouldn't have blamed Ithiel for taking a woman out to dinner now and then in Washington. He needed plain, ordinary quiet times. I turned on so much power in those days. Especially after midnight, my favorite time to examine my psyche—what love was; and death; and hell and eternal punishment; and what Ithiel was going to cost me in the judgment of God when I closed my eyes on this world forever. All my revivalist emotions came out after one A.M., whole nights of tears, anguish and hysteria. I drove him out of his head. To put a stop to this, he'd have to marry me. Then he'd never again have to worry. All my demon power would be at his service. But meanwhile if he got an hour's sleep toward morning and time enough to shave before his first appointment, he'd swallow his coffee, saying that he looked like Lazarus in his shroud. He was vain of his good looks too," said Clara to Ms. Wong. "Maybe that's why I chose that kind of punishment, to put rings under his eyes. Once he said that he had to outline a piece of legislation for the Fiat people—they were trying to get a bill passed in

Congress—and they'd think he'd spent the night at an orgy and now couldn't get his act together."

Clara wasn't about to tell Teddy that in Milan when Mike Spontini had invited her to sit in front with him, she had found the palm of his hand waiting for her on the seat, and she had lifted herself up immediately and given him her evening bag to hold. In the dark his fingers soon closed on her thigh. Then she pushed in the cigarette lighter and he guessed what she would do with it when the coil was hot, so he stopped, he let her be. You didn't mention such incidents to the man you were with. It was anyway commonplace stuff to a man who thought world politics continually.

In the accounts heard by Ms. Wong (who had so much American sensitivity, despite her air of Oriental distance and the Chinese cut of her clothes), Clara's frankness may have made *her* seem foreign. Clara went beyond the conventions of American openness. The emerald ring appeased her for a time, but Ithiel was not inclined to move forward, and Clara became more difficult. She told him she had decided that they would be buried in the same grave. She said, "I'd rather go into the ground with the man I loved than share a bed with somebody indifferent. Yes, I think we should be in the same coffin. Or two coffins, but the one who dies last will be on the top. Side by side is also possible. Holding hands, if that could be arranged." Another frequent topic was the sex and the name of their first child. An Old Testament name was what she preferred—Zebulon or Gad or Asher or Naf-

tali. For a girl, Michal, perhaps, or Naomi. He vetoed
Michal because she had mocked David for his naked
victory dance, and then he refused to take part in such
talk at all. He didn't want to make any happy plans. He
was glum with her when she said that there was a lovely
country cemetery back in Indiana with big horse chest-
nuts all around.

When he went off to South America on business, she
learned from Etta Wolfenstein that he had taken a Washington secretary with him for assistance and (knowing
Teddy) everything else. To show him what was what,
Clara had an affair with a young Jean-Claude just over
from Paris, and within a week he was sharing her apartment. He was very good-looking, but he seldom washed.
His dirt was so ingrained that she couldn't get him clean
in the shower stall. She had to take a room at the Plaza
to force him into the tub. Then for a while she could
bear the smell of him. He appealed to her to help get a
work permit, and she took him to Steinsalz, Ithiel's lawyer. Later Jean-Claude refused to return her house key,
and she had to go to Steinsalz again. "Have your lock
changed, dear girl," said Steinsalz, and he asked whether
she wanted Ithiel billed for these consultations. He was
a friend and admired Ithiel.

"But Ithiel told me you never charged him for your
services."

Clara had discovered how amused New Yorkers were
by her ignorance.

"Since you took up with this Frenchie, have you missed anything around the house?"

She seemed slow to understand, but that was simply a put-on. She had locked the emerald ring in her deposit box (this, too, an act suggestive of burial).

She said firmly, "Jean-Claude is no bum."

Steinsalz liked Clara too, for her passionate character. Somehow he knew, also, that her family had money—a real-estate fortune, and this gained her a certain consideration with him. Jean-Claude was not the Steinsalz type. He advised Clara to patch up her differences with Ithiel. "Not to use sex for spite," he said. Clara could not help but look at the lawyer's lap, where because he was obese his sex organ was outlined by the pressure of his fat. It made her think of one of those objects that appeared when art-lovers on their knees made rubbings on a church floor. The figure of a knight dead for centuries.

"Then why can't Ithiel stay faithful?"

Steinsalz's first name was Bobby. He was a great economist. He ran a million-dollar practice, and it cost him not a cent. He sublet a corner office space from a flashy accountant and paid him in legal advice.

Steinsalz said, "Teddy is a genius. If he didn't prefer to hang loose, he could name his position in Washington. He values his freedom, so that when he wanted to visit Mr. Leakey in the Olduvai Gorge, he just picked up and went. He thinks no more about going to Iran than I do about Coney Island. The Shah likes to talk to him. He

sent for him once just to be briefed on Kissinger. I tell
you this, Clara, so that you won't hold Ithiel on too short
a leash. He truly appreciates you, but he irks easy. A
little consideration of his needs would fill him with gratitude. A good idea is not to get too clamorous around
him. Let me tell you, there are curators in the zoo who
give more thought to the needs of a fruit bat than any
of us give our fellowman."

Clara answered him, "There are animals who come in
pairs. So suppose the female pines?"

That was a good talk, and Clara remembered Steinsalz
gratefully.

"Everybody knows how to advise lovers," said Steinsalz. "But only the lovers can say what's what."

A bookish bachelor, he lived with his eighty-year-old
mother, who had to be taken to the toilet in her wheel-
chair. He liked to list the famous men he had gone to
high school with—Holz the philosopher, Buchman the
Nobel physicist, Lashover the crystallographer. "And
yours truly, whose appellate briefs have made legal history."

Clara said, "I sort of loved old Steinsalz too. He was
like a Santa Claus with an empty sack who comes down
your chimney to steal everything in the house—that's
one of Ithiel's wisecracks, about Steinsalz and property.
In his own off-the-wall way, Steinsalz was generous."

Clara took advice from the lawyer and made peace
with Ithiel on his return. Then the same mistakes over-
took them. "I was a damn recidivist. When Jean-Claude

left I was glad of it. Getting into the tub with him at the Plaza was a kind of frolic—a private camp event. They say the Sun King stank. If so, Jean-Claude could have gone straight to the top of Versailles. But my family are cleanliness freaks. Before she would sit in your car, my Granny would force you to whisk-broom the seat, under the floor mat too, to make sure her serge wouldn't pick up any dust." By the way, Clara locked up the ring not for fear that Jean-Claude would steal it but to protect it from contamination by her wrongful behavior in bed.

But when Ithiel came back, his relations with Clara were not what they had been. Two outside parties had come between them, even though Ithiel seemed indifferent to Jean-Claude. Jealous and hurt, Clara could not forgive the little twit from Washington, of whom Etta Wolfenstein had given her a full picture. That girl was stupid but had very big boobs. When Ithiel talked about his mission to Betancourt in Venezuela, Clara was unimpressed. An American woman in love was far more important than any South American hotshot. "And did you take your little helper along to the president's palace to show off her chest development?"

Ithiel sensibly said, "Let's not beat on each other too much," and Clara repented and agreed. But soon she set up another obstacle course of tests and rules, and asserted herself unreasonably. When Ithiel had his hair cut, Clara said, "That's not the way I like it, but then I'm not the one you're pleasing." She'd say, "You're grooming yourself more than you used to. I'm sure Jascha Heifetz doesn't take such care of his hands." She made mistakes. You didn't send a man with eyes from Greek mythology to the bathroom to cut his fingernails, even if you did have a horror of clippings on the carpet—she'd forget that she and Ithiel were the Human Pair.

But at the time she couldn't be sure that Ithiel was thinking as she did about "Human." To sound him out, she assumed a greater interest in politics and got him to talk about Africa, China and Russia. What emerged was the insignificance of the personal factor. Clara repeated and tried out words like Kremlin or Lubyanka in her mind (they sounded like the living end) while she heard Ithiel tell of people who couldn't explain why they were in prison, never rid of lice and bedbugs, never free from dysentery and TB, and finally hallucinating. They make an example of them, she thought, to show that nobody is anybody, everybody is expendable. And even here, when Ithiel was pushed to say it, he admitted that here in the U.S., the status of the individual was weakening and probably in irreversible decline. Felons getting special consideration was a sign of it. He could be remote about such judgments, as if his soul were one of a dozen similar souls in a jury box, hearing evidence: to find us innocent would be nice, but guilty couldn't shock him much. She concluded that he was in a dangerous moral state and that it was up to her to rescue him from it. The Human Pair was also a rescue operation.

"A terrible crisis threatened to pinch us both to death."

At the time, she was not advanced enough to think this to a conclusion. Later she would have known how to put it: You couldn't separate love from being. You could Be, even though you were alone. But in that case, you loved only yourself. If so, everybody else was a phantom, and then world politics was a shadow play. Therefore she, Clara, was the only key to politics that Ithiel was likely to find. Otherwise he might as well stop bothering his head about his grotesque game theories, ideology, treaties, and the rest of it. Why bother to line up so many phantoms?

But this was not a time for things to go well. He missed the point, although it was as big as a boulder to her. They had bad arguments—"It was a mistake not to let him sleep"—and after a few oppressive months, he made plans to leave the country with yet another of his outlandish lady friends.

Clara heard, again from Etta Wolfenstein, that Ithiel was staying in a fleabag hotel in the Forties west of Broadway, where he'd be hard to find. " 'Safety in sleaze,' Etta said—S*he* was a piece of work." He was to meet the new girlfriend at Kennedy next afternoon.

At once Clara went uptown in a cab and walked into the cramped lobby, dirty tile like a public lavatory. She pressed with both hands on the desk and lied that she was Ithiel's wife, saying that he had sent her to check him out and take his luggage. "They believed me. You're never so cool as when you're burned up completely. They didn't even ask for identification, since I paid cash and tipped everybody five bucks apiece. When I went upstairs

I was astonished that he could bring himself to sit down on such a bed, much less sleep in those grungy sheets. The morgue would have been nicer."

Then she returned to her apartment with his suitcase—the one they took to Cortina, where she had been so happy. She waited until after dark, and he turned up at about seven o'clock. Cool with her, which meant that he was boiling.

"Where do you get off, pulling this on me?"

"You didn't say you were coming to New York. You were sneaking out of the country."

"Since when do I have to punch the clock in and out like an employee!"

She stood up to him without fear. In fact she was desperate. She shouted at him the Old Testament names of their unborn children. "You're betraying Michal and Naomi."

As a rule, Ithiel was self-possessed to an unusual degree, "unless we were making love. It was cold anger at first," as Clara was to tell it. "He spoke like a man in a three-piece suit. I reminded him that the destiny of both our races depended on those children. I said they were supposed to be a merger of two high types. I'm not against other types, but they'd be there anyway, and more numerous—I'm no racist."

"I can't have you check me out of my hotel and take my suitcase. Nobody is going to supervise me. And I suppose you went through my things."

"I wouldn't do that. I was protecting you. You're making the mistake of your life."

At that moment Clara's look was hollow. You saw the bones of her face, especially the orbital ones. The inflammation of her eyes would have shocked Ithiel if he hadn't been bent on teaching her a lesson. Time to draw the line, was what he was saying to himself.

"You're not going back to that horrible hotel!" she said when he picked up his bag.

"I have a reservation in another place."

"Teddy, take off your coat. Don't go now, I'm in a bad way. I love you with my soul." She said it again, when the door swung shut after him.

He told himself it would set a bad precedent to let her control him with her fits.

The luxury of the Park Avenue room didn't sit well with him—the gilded wall fixtures, the striped upholstery, the horror of the fresco painting, the bed turned back like the color photograph in the brochure, with two tablets of chocolate mint on the night table. The bathroom was walled with mirrors, the brightwork shone, and he felt the life going out of him. He went to the bed and sat on the edge but did not lie down. It was not in the cards for him to sleep that night. The phone rang—it was a mean sound, a thin rattle—and Etta said, "Clara has swallowed a bottle of sleeping pills. She called me and I sent the ambulance. You'd better go to Bellevue; you may be needed. Are you alone there?"

He went immediately to the hospital, hurrying through gray corridors, stopping to ask directions until he found himself in the waiting space for relatives and friends, by a narrow horizontal window. He saw bodies on stretchers, no one resembling Clara. A young man in a dog collar presently joined him. He said he was Clara's minister.

"I didn't realize that she had one."

"She often comes to talk to me. Yes, she's in my parish."

"Has her stomach been pumped?"

"That—oh, yes. But she took a big dose, and they're not certain yet. You're Ithiel Regler, I suppose?"

"I am."

The young minister asked no other questions. No discussions occurred. You couldn't help but be thankful for his tact. Also for the information he brought from the nurses. Word came in the morning that she would live. They were moving her upstairs to a women's ward.

When she was able, she sent word through her clergyman friend that she didn't want to see Ithiel, had no wish to hear from him, ever. After a day of self-torment in the luxury of the hotel on Park Avenue, he canceled his trip to Europe. He fended off the sympathy of Etta Wolfenstein, avid to hear about his torments, and went back to Washington. The clergyman made a point of seeing him off at Penn Station. There he was, extra tall, in his dickey and clerical collar. Baldness had just come over him, he had decided not to wear a hat, and he kept reaching for vanished or vanishing tufts of hair. Ithiel was made uncomfortable by his sympathy. Because the young man had nothing at all to tell him except that he shouldn't blame himself. He may have been saying: "You with your sins, your not very good heart. I with my hair loss." This took no verbal form. Only a mute urgency in his decent face. He said, "She's ambulatory already. She goes around the ward and tapes back their IV needles when they work loose. She's a help to old derelicts."

You can always get a remedy, you can tap into solace when you need it, you can locate a mental fix. America is generous in this regard. The air is full of helpful hints. Ithiel was too proud to accept any handy fix. Like: "Suicide is a power move." "Suicide is punitive." "The poor kids never mean it." "It's all the drama of rescue." You could tell yourself such things; they didn't mean a damn. In all the world, now, there wasn't a civilized place left where a woman would say, "I love you with my soul." Only this backcountry girl was that way still. If no more mystical sacredness remained in the world, she hadn't been informed yet. Straight-nosed Ithiel, heading for Washington and the Capitol dome, symbolic of a nation swollen with world significance, set a greater value on Clara than on anything in *this* place, or any place. He thought, This is what I opted for, and this is what I deserve. Walking into that room at the Regency, I got what I had coming.

It was after this that Clara's marriages began—first the church wedding in her granny's gown, the arrangements elaborate, Tiffany engravings, Limoges china, Lalique glassware. Mom and Dad figured that after two suicide attempts, the fullest effort must be made to provide a stable life for their Clara. They were dear about it. There were no economies. Husband One was an educational psychologist who tested schoolchildren. His name was a good one—Monserrat. On the stationery she had printed, Clara was Mme de Monserrat. But as she was to say to Ithiel: "This marriage was like a Thanksgiving turkey. After a month the bird is drying out and you're still eating breast of turkey. It needs more and more Russian dressing, and pretty soon the sharpest knife in the city won't slice it." If there was anything she could do to perfection, it was to invent such descriptions. "Pretty soon you're trying to eat threads of bird meat," she said.

Her second husband was a Southern boy who went to Congress and even ran in a few presidential primaries. They lived out in Virginia for about a year, and she saw something of Ithiel in Washington. She was not very kind to him then. "Frankly," she told him at lunch one day, "I can't imagine why I ever wanted to embrace you. I look at you, and I say, Yuch!"

"There probably is a *yuch* aspect to me," said Ithiel, perfectly level. "It does no harm to learn about your repulsive side."

She couldn't flap him. In the glance she then gave him, there was a glimmer of respect.

"I was a little crazy," she would say later.

At that time she and her Southern husband were trying to have a child. She telephoned Ithiel and described the difficulties they were having. "I thought maybe you would oblige me," she said.

"Out of the question. It would be grotesque."

"A child with classic Greek eyes. Listen, Teddy, as I sit here, what do you think I'm doing to myself? Where do you suppose my hand is, and what am I touching?"

"I've already done my bit for the species," he said. "Why breed more sinners?"

"What do you suggest?"

"These utility husbands are not the answer."

"But for you and me, it wasn't in the cards, Ithiel. Why did you have so many women?"

"For you there were quite a few men—maybe it has something to do with democracy. There are so many eligibles, such handsome choices. Mix with your equals. And why limit yourself?"

"Okay, but it comes out so unhappy. . . . And why shouldn't I be pregnant by you? Alistair and I aren't compatible that way. Haven't you forgiven me for what I said that day about your being *yuch*? I was just being perverse. Ithiel, if you were here now . . ."

"But I'm not going to be."

"Just for procreation. There are even surrogate mothers these days."

"I can see a black dude motorcycle messenger in boots, belt and helmet, waiting with a warm box for the condom full of sperm. 'Here you are, Billy. Rush this to the lady.' "

"You shouldn't make fun. You should think of the old Stoic who told his buddies when they caught him in the act, 'Mock not, I plant a Man.' Oh, I talk this way to make an impression on you. It's not real. I ask you—and now I'm serious—what should I do?"

"It should be Alistair's child."

But she divorced Alistair and married Mike Spontini, whom she had threatened in Milan to burn with the dashboard lighter coil. For Spontini she had real feeling, she said. "Even though I caught him humping another woman just before we were married."

"He wasn't meant to be a husband."

"I thought once he got to know my quality I'd mean more to him. He'd finally *see* it. I don't say that I'm better than other women. I'm not superior. I'm nutty, also. But I am in touch with the *me* in myself. There's so much I could do for a man that I loved. How *could* Mike, in my bed, with the door unlocked and me in the house, ball such an awful tramp as that? *Tell* me."

"Well, people have to be done with disorder, finally, and by the time they're done they're also finished. When they back off to take a new leap, they realize they've torn too many ligaments. It's all over."

Mike Spontini intended to do right by Clara. He bought a handsome place in Connecticut with a view of the sea.

He never invested badly, never lost a penny. He doubled his money in Connecticut. The Fifth Avenue apartment was a good deal too. In the country, Clara became a gardener. She must have hoped that there was sympathetic magic in flowers and vegetables, or that the odor of soil would calm Mike's jetting soul, bring down his fever. The marriage lasted three years. He paid the wretchedness fee, he did bad time, as convicts say, then he filed for divorce and liquidated the real estate. It took a stroke to stop Mad Mike. The left side of his face was disfigured in such a manner (this was Clara speaking) that it became a fixed commentary on the life strategy he had followed: "his failed concept." But Clara was strong on loyalty, and she was loyal even to a stricken ex-husband. You don't cut all bonds after years of intimacy. After his stroke, she arranged a birthday party for him at the hospital; she sent a cake to the room. However, the doctor asked her not to come.

When you were down, busted, blasted, burnt out, dying, you saw the best of Clara.

So it was odd that she should also have become an executive, highly paid and influential. She could make fashionable talk, she dressed with originality, she knew a lot and at first hand about decadence, but at any moment she could set aside the "czarina" and become the hayseed, the dupe of traveling salesmen or grifters who wanted to lure her up to the hayloft. In her you might see suddenly a girl from a remote town, from the vestigial America of one-room schoolhouses, constables, covered-dish suppers, one of those communities bypassed by technology and urban development. Her father, remember, was still a vestryman, and her mother sent checks to TV fundamentalists. In a sophisticated boardroom Clara could be as plain as cornmeal mush, and in such a mood, when she opened her mouth, you couldn't guess whether she would speak or blow bubble gum. Yet anybody who had it in mind to get around her was letting himself in for lots of bad news.

She was prepared always to acknowledge total ignorance, saying, as she had so often said to Ithiel Regler, "*Tell* me!" The girl from the backwoods was also sentimental; she kept souvenirs, family photographs, lace valentines, and she cherished the ring Ithiel had bought her. She held on to it through four marriages. When she had it appraised for insurance, she found that it had become very valuable. It was covered for fifteen thousand dollars. Ithiel had never been smart about money. He was a bad investor—unlucky, careless. On Forty-seventh Street twenty years ago, Madison Hamilton had goofed, uncharacteristically, in pricing his emerald. But Clara was careless as well, for the ring disappeared while she was carrying Patsy. Forgotten on a washstand, maybe, or stolen from a bench at the tennis club. The loss depressed her; her depression deepened as she searched for it in handbags, drawers, upholstery crevices, shag rugs, pill bottles.

Laura Wong remembered how upset Clara had been.

"*That* put you back on the couch," she said, with Oriental gentleness.

Clara had been hoping to free herself from Dr. Gladstone. She had said as much. "Now that I'm expecting for the third time I should be able to go it alone at last. A drink with Ithiel when I'm low does more for me. I've already got more doctors than any woman should need. Gladstone will ask me why this Ithiel symbol should still be so powerful. And what will there be to say? When the bag of your Hoover fills with dust, you replace it with another. Why not get rid of feeling-dust too. Yet . . . even a technician like Gladstone knows better. What he wants is to desensitize me. I was ready to die for love. Okay, I'm still living, have a husband, expect another baby. I'm as those theology people say, all those divinity fudges: *situated*. If, finally, you get situated, why go into mourning over a ring?"

In the end Clara did telephone Ithiel to tell him about the emerald. "Such a link between us," she said. "And it makes me guilty to bother you with it now, when things aren't going well for you with Francine."

"Never so bad that I can't spare some words of support," said Ithiel, so dependable. He disliked grieving over his own troubles. And he was so highly organized—as if living up to the classic balance of his face; such a pair of eyes seemed to call for a particular, maybe even an administered, sort of restraint. Ithiel could be hard on himself. He blamed himself about Clara and for his failed marriages, including the present one. And yet the choices he made showed him to be reckless too. He was committed to high civility, structure, order; nevertheless he took chances with women, he was a gambler, something of an anarchist. There was anarchy on both sides. Nevertheless, his attachment, his feeling for her was—to his own surprise—permanent. His continually increasing respect for her came over the horizon like a moon taking decades to rise.

"Seven marriages between us, and we still love each other," she said. Ten years before, it would have been a risky thing to say, it would have stirred a gust of fear in him. Now she was sure that he would agree, as indeed he did.

"That is true."

"How do you interpret the ring, then?"

"I don't," said Ithiel. "It's a pretty bad idea to wring what happens to get every drop of meaning out of it. The way people twist their emotional laundry is not to be believed. *I* don't feel that you wronged me by losing that ring. You say it was insured?"

"Damn right."

"Then file a claim. The companies charge enough. Your premiums must be out of sight."

"I'm really torn up about it," said Clara.

"That's your tenth-century soul. Much your doctor can do about that!"

"He helps, in some respects."

"Those guys!" said Ithiel. "If a millipede came into

the office, he'd leave with an infinitesimal crutch for each leg."

Reporting this conversation to Ms. Wong, Clara said, "That did it. That's the anarchist in Ithiel busting out. It gives me such a boost to chat with him even for five minutes."

The insurance company paid her fifteen thousand dollars, and then, a year later, the missing ring turned up.

In one of her fanatical fits of spring cleaning, she found it beneath the bed, above the caster, held in the frame to which the small braking lever was attached. It was on her side of the bed. She must have been groping for a paper tissue and knocked it off the bedside table. For what purpose she had been groping, now that it was discovered, she didn't care to guess. She held the ring to her face, felt actually as if she were inhaling the green essence of this ice—no, ice was diamond; still, this emerald also was an ice. In it Ithiel's pledge was frozen. Or else it represented the permanent form of the passion she had had for this man. The hot form would have been red, like a node inside the body, in the sexual parts. That you'd see as a ruby. The cool form was this concentrate of clear green. This was not one of her fancies; it was as real as the green of the ocean, as the mountains in whose innards such gems are mined. She thought these locations (the Atlantic, the Andes) as she thought the inside of her own body. In her summary fashion, she said, "Maybe what it comes to is that I am an infant mine." She had three small girls to prove it.

The insurance company was not notified. Clara was not prepared to return the money. By now it simply wasn't there. It had been spent on a piano, a carpet, yet another set of Limoges china—God knows what else. So the ring couldn't be reinsured, but that didn't matter much. Exultingly glad, she told Ithiel on the telephone, "*In*credible, where that ring fell! Right under me, as I lay there suffering over it. I could have touched it by dropping my arm. I could have poked it with my finger."

"How many of us can say anything like that?" said Ithiel. "That you can lie in bed and have the cure for what ails you within reach."

"Only you don't know it . . ." said Clara. "I thought you'd be pleased."

"Oh, I am. I think it's great. It's like adding ten years to your life to have it back."

"I'll have to take double good care of it. It's not insurable. . . . I'm never sure how important an item like this ring can be to a man who has to think about the Atlantic Alliance and all that other stuff. Deterrence, theater nuclear forces . . . completely incomprehensible to me."

"If only the answers were under my bed," said Ithiel. "But you shouldn't think I can't take a ring seriously, or that I'm so snooty about world significance or Lenin's 'decisive correlation of forces'—that you're just a kid and I indulge you like a big daddy. I like you better than I do the president, or the national security adviser."

"Yes, I can see that, and why, humanly, you'd rather have me to deal with."

"Just think, if you didn't do your own spring cleaning, your help might have found the ring."

"My help wouldn't dream of going under the bed at any season of the year; that's why I took time off from the office. I had to work around Wilder, who's been reading John le Carré. Sitting in the middle of his female household like a Sioux Indian in his wickiup. Like Sitting Bull. All the same, he's often very sweet. Even when he acts like the reigning male. And he'd be totally at sea if I weren't . . . oops!"

"If you weren't manning the ship," said Ithiel.

Well, it was a feminine household, and for that reason perhaps Gina felt less foreign in New York. She said that she loved the city, it had so many accommodations for women specifically. Everybody who arrived, moreover, already knew the place because of movies and magazines, and when John Kennedy said he was a Berliner, all of Berlin could have answered, "So? We are New Yorkers." There was no such thing as being strange here, in Gina's opinion.

"That's what *you* think, baby," was Clara's response, although it was not made to Gina Wegman, it was made to Ms. Wong. "And let's hope she never finds out what this town can do to a young person. But when you think about such a pretty child and the Italian charm of her looks, so innocent—although innocence is a tricky thing to prove. You can't expect her to forget about being a girl just because the surroundings are so dangerous."

"Do you let her ride the subway?"

"*Let* her!" said Clara. "When the young things go into the street, where's your control over them? All I can do is pray she'll be safe. I told her if she was going to wear a short skirt she should also put on a coat. But what good is advice without a slum background? What a woman needs today is some slum experience. However, it's up to me to keep an eye on the child, and I must assume she's innocent and doesn't *want* to be rubbed up against in the rush hours by dirty-sex delinquents."

"It's hard to be in the responsible-adult position," said Laura.

"It's the old-time religion in me. Stewardship." Clara said this partly in fun. Yet when she invoked her background, her formative years, she became for a moment the girl with the wide forehead, the large eyes, the smallish nose, who had been forced by her parents to memorize long passages from Galatians and Corinthians.

"She suits the children," said Ms. Wong.

"They're very comfortable with her, and there's no strain with Lucy." For Clara, Lucy was the main thing. At this stage she was so sullen—overweight, shy of making friends, jealous, resistant, troubled. Hard to move. Clara had often suggested that Lucy's hair be cut, the heavy curls that bounded her face. "The child has hair

like Jupiter," said Clara in one of her sessions with Laura.
"Sometimes I think she must be as strong—potentially—
as a hod carrier."

"Wouldn't she like it short and trim, like yours?"

"I don't want a storm over it," said Clara.

The child was clumsy certainly (although her legs were
going to be good—you could already see that). But there
was a lot of power under this clumsiness. Lucy com-
plained that her little sisters united against her. It looked
that way, Clara agreed. Patsy and Selma were graceful
children, and they made Lucy seem burly, awkward before the awkward age. She would be awkward after it
too, just as her mother had been, and eruptive, defiant
and prickly. When Clara got through to her (the super-
large eyes of her slender face had to bear down on the
kid till she opened up—"You can always talk to Mother
about what goes on, what's cooking inside"), then Lucy
sobbed that all the girls in her class snubbed and made
fun of her.

"Little bitches," said Clara to Ms. Wong. "Amazing
how early it all starts. Even Selma and Patsy, affectionate
kids, are developing at Lucy's expense. Her 'grossness'—
you know what a word 'gross' is with children—makes
ladies of them. And the little sisters are far from dumb,
but I believe Lucy is the one with the brains. There's
something *major* in Lucy. Gina Wegman agrees with me.
Lucy acts like a small she-brute. It's not just that Roman
hairdo. She's greedy and bears grudges. God, she does!
That's where Gina comes in, because Gina has so much

class, and Gina *likes* her. As much as I can, with executive responsibilities and bearing the brunt of the household, I mother those girls. Also, I have sessions with the school psychologists—I was once married to one of those characters—and discussions with other mothers. Maybe putting them in the 'best' schools is a big mistake. The influence of the top stockbrokers and lawyers in town has to be overcome there. I'm saying it as I see it. . . ."

What Clara couldn't say, because Laura Wong's upbringing was so different from her own (and it was her own that seemed the more alien), had to do with Matthew 16:18: "the gates of hell shall not prevail against it"—*it* being love, against which no door can be closed. This was more of the primitive stuff that Clara had brought from the backcountry and was part of her confused inner life. Explaining it to her confidante would be more trouble than it was worth, if you considered that in the end Ms. Wong would still be in the dark—the second dark being darker than the first. Here Clara couldn't say it as she saw it.

"There's a lot of woman in that child. A handsome, powerful woman. Gina Wegman intuits the same about her," said Clara.

She was much drawn to Gina, only it wouldn't be wise to make a younger friend of her; that would lie too close to adoption and perhaps cause rivalry with the children. You had to keep your distance—avoid intimacies, avoid confidences especially. Yet there was nothing wrong with an occasional treat, as long as the treat was educational. For instance, you asked the au pair girl to bring some papers to your office, and then you could show her around the suite, give her a nice tea. She let Gina attend a trade briefing on shoulder pads and hear arguments for this or that type of padding, the degree of the lift, the desirability of a straighter line in the hang of one's clothes; the new trends in size in the designs of Armani, Christian Lacroix, Sonia Rykiel. She took the girl to a show of the latest spring fashions from Italy, where she heard lots of discussion about the desirability of over-the-knee boots, and of the layering of the skirts of Gianni Versace over puffy knickers. Agitprop spokesmen putting across short garments of puckered silk, or jackets of cunningly imitated ocelot, or simulated beaver capes—all this the ingenious work of millionaire artisans, billionaire designer commissars. Gina came suitably dressed, a pretty girl, very young. Clara couldn't say how this fashion display impressed her. It was best, Clara thought, to underplay the whole show: the luxurious setting, the star cast of Italians, and the pomp of the experts—somewhat subdued by the presence of the impassive czarina.

"Well, what should I say about these things?" said Clara, again confiding to Laura Wong. "This glitter is our living, and nice women grow old and glum, cynical too, in all this glitz of fur, silk, leather, cosmetics, et cetera, of the glamour trades. Meanwhile my family responsibilities are what count. How to protect my children."

"And you wanted to give your Gina a treat," said Ms. Wong.

"And I'm glad about the playfulness," said Clara. "We have to have that. But the sums it costs! And who gets what! Besides, Laura, if it has to be slathered onto women . . . If a woman is beautiful and you add beautiful dress, that's one thing: you're adding beauty to beauty. But if the operation comes from the outside only, it has curious effects. And that's the way it generally happens. Of course there will be barefaced schemers or people in despair looking glorious. But in most cases of decoration, the effect is hell. It's a variation on that Auden line I love so much about 'the will of the insane to suffer.' " When she had said this she looked blankly violent. She had gone farther than she had intended, farther than Ms. Wong was prepared to follow. Here Clara might well have added the words from Matthew 16.

Her Chinese-American confidante was used to such sudden zooming. Clara was not being stagy when she expressed such ideas about clothing; she was brooding audibly, and very often she had Ithiel Regler in mind, the women he had gone off with, the women he had married. Among them were several "fancy women"—she meant that they were overdressed sexpots, gaudy and dizzy, "ground-dragging titzers," on whom a man like Ithiel should never have squandered his substance. And he had been married three times and had two children. What a waste! Why should there have been seven mar-

riages, five children! Even Mike Spontini, for all his pow-
ers and attractions, had been a waste—a Mediterranean,
an Italian husband who came back to his wife when he
saw fit, that is, when he was tired of business and of
playing around. *All* the others had been dummy husbands, humanly unserious—you could get no real masculine resonance out of any of them.

What a pity! thought Laura Wong. Teddy Regler should
have married Clara. Apply any measure—need, sympathy, feeling, you name it—and the two profiles (that
was the Wong woman's way of putting it) were just about
identical. And Ithiel was doing very badly now. Just after
Gina became her au pair girl, Clara learned from the
Wolfenstein woman, Teddy's first wife, who had her scouts
in Washington, that the third Mrs. Regler had hired a
moving van and emptied the house one morning as soon
as Teddy left for the office. Coming home in the evening,
he found nothing but the bed they had shared the night
before (stripped of bedding) and a few insignificant kitchen
items. Francine, the third wife, had had no child to take
care of. She had spent her days wandering around department stores. That much was true. He didn't let her
feel that she was sharing his life. Yet the man was stunned,
wiped out—depressed, then ill. He had been mourning
his mother. Francine had made her move a week after
his mother's funeral. One week to the day.

Clara and Laura together had decided that Francine
couldn't bear his grieving. She had no such emotions
herself, and she disliked them. "Some people just can't

grasp grief," was what Clara said. Possibly, too, there was another man in the picture, and it would have been awkward, after an afternoon with this man, to come home to a husband absorbed in dark thoughts or needing consolation. "I can easily picture this from the wife's side," said Laura. Her own divorce had been a disagreeable one. Her husband, a man named Odo Fenger, a dermatologist, had been one of those ruddy, blond, fleshy baby-men who have to engross you in their emotions (eyes changing from baby blue to whiskey blue) and so centuple the agonies of breaking away. So why *not* send a van to the house and move straight into the future—future being interpreted as never (never in this life) meeting the other party again. "That Francine didn't have it in her to see him through, after the feeling had been killed out of *her*. Each age has its own way of dealing with these things. As you said before, in the Renaissance you used poison. When the feeling is killed, the other party becomes physically unbearable."

Clara didn't entirely attend to what Laura was saying. Her only comment was, "I suppose there *has* been progress. Better moving than murdering. At least both parties go on living."

By now Ms. Wong wanted no husbands, no children. She had withdrawn from all that. But she respected Clara Velde. Perhaps her curiosity was even deeper than her respect, and she was most curious about Clara and Ithiel Regler. She collected newspaper clippings about Regler and like Wilder Velde didn't miss his TV interviews, if she could help it.

When Clara heard about Francine and her moving van, she flew down to Washington as soon as she could get to the shuttle. Gina was there to take charge of the children. Clara never felt so secure as when dependable Gina was looking after them. As a backup Clara had Mrs. Peralta, the cleaning woman, who had also become a family friend.

Clara found Ithiel in a state of sick dignity. He was affectionate with her but reserved about his troubles, thanked her somewhat formally for her visit, and told her that he would rather not go into the history of his relations with Francine.

"Just as you like," said Clara. "But you haven't got anybody here; there's just me in New York. I'll look after you if you should need it."

"I'm glad you've come. I've been despondent. What I've learned, though, is that when people get to talking about their private troubles, they go into a winding spiral about relationships, and they absolutely stupefy everybody with boredom. I'm sure that I can turn myself around."

"Of course. You're resilient," said Clara, proud of him. "So we won't say too much about it. Only, that woman didn't have to wait until your mother was dead. She might have done it earlier. You don't wait until a man is down, then dump on him."

"Shall we have a good dinner? Middle Eastern, Chinese, Italian or French? I see you're wearing the emerald."

"I hoped you'd notice. Now tell me, Ithiel, are you giving up your place? Did she leave it very bare?"

"I can camp there until some money comes in and then refit the living room."

"There ought to be somebody taking care of you."

"If there's one thing I can do without, it's this picture of poor me, deep in the dumps, and some faithful female who makes my heart swell with gratitude." Being rigorous with his heart gave him satisfaction.

"He likes to look at the human family as it is," Clara was to explain.

"You wouldn't marry a woman who did value you," said Clara at dinner. "Like Groucho Marx saying he wouldn't join a club that accepted him for membership."

"Let me tell you," said Ithiel, and she understood that he had drawn back to the periphery in order to return to the center from one of his strange angles. "When the president has to go to Walter Reed Hospital for surgery and the papers are full of sketches of his bladder and his prostate—I can remember the horrible drawings of Eisenhower's ileitis—then I'm glad there are no diagrams of my vitals in the press and the great public isn't staring at my anus. For the same reason, I've always discouraged small talk about my psyche. It's only fair that Francine shouldn't have valued me. I would have lived out the rest of my life with her. I was patient. . . ."

"You mean you gave up, you resigned yourself."

"I was affectionate," Ithiel insisted.

"You had to fake it. You saw your mistake and were ready to pay for it. She didn't give a squat for your affection."

"I was faithful."

"No, you were licked," said Clara. "You went to your office hideaway and did your thing about Russia or Iran. Those crazy characters from Libya or Lebanon are *some* fun to follow. What did she do for fun?"

"I suppose that every morning she had to decide where to go with her credit cards. She liked auctions and furniture shows. She bought an ostrich-skin outfit, complete with boots and purse."

"What else did she do for fun?"

Ithiel was silent and reserved, moving crumbs back and forth with the blade of his knife. Clara thought, She cheated on him. Precious Francine had no idea what a husband she had. And what did it matter what a woman like that did with her gross organs. Clara didn't get a rise out of Ithiel with her suggestive question. She might just as well have been talking to one of those Minoans dug up by Evans or Schliemann or whoever, characters like those in the silent films, painted with eye-lengthening makeup. If Clara was from the Middle Ages, Ithiel was from antiquity. Imagine a low-down woman who felt that *he* didn't appreciate *her*! Why, Ithiel could be the Gibbon or the Tacitus of the American Empire. *He* wouldn't have thought it, but she remembered to this day how he would speak about Keynes's sketches of Clemenceau, Lloyd George and Woodrow Wilson. If he wanted, he could do with Nixon, Johnson, Kennedy or Kissinger, with the Shah or de Gaulle, what Keynes had done with the Allies at Versailles. World figures had found Ithiel worth their while. Sometimes he let slip a comment or a judgment: "Neither the Russians nor the Americans can manage the world. Not capable of organizing the future." When she came into her own, Clara thought, she'd set up a fund for him so he could write his views.

She said, "If you'd like me to stay over, Wilder has gone to Minnesota to see some peewee politician who needs a set of speeches. Gina is entertaining a few friends at the house."

"Do I look as if I needed friendly first aid?"

"You are *down*. What's the disgrace in that?"

Ithiel drove her to the airport. For the moment the parkways were empty. Ahead were airport lights, and in the slanting planes seated travelers by the thousands came in, went up.

Clara asked what job he was doing. "Not who you're doing it for, but the subject."

He said he was making a survey of the opinions of émigrés on the new Soviet regime—he seemed glad to change the subject, although he had always been a bit reluctant to talk politics to her. Politics were not her thing, he didn't like to waste words on uncomprehending idle questioners, but he seemed to have his emotional reasons tonight for saying just what it was that he was up to. "Some of the smartest émigrés are saying that the Russians didn't announce liberalization until they had crushed the dissidents. Then they co-opted the dissidents' ideas. After you've gotten rid of your enemies, you're ready to abolish capital punishment—that's how Alexander Zinoviev puts it. And it wasn't only the KGB that destroyed the dissident movement but the whole party organization, and the party was supported by the Soviet people. They strangled the opposition, and now they're pretending to be *it*. You have the Soviet leaders themselves criticizing Soviet society. When it has to be done, they take over. And the West is thrilled by all the reforms."

"So we're going to be bamboozled again," said Clara.

But there were other matters, more pressing, to discuss on the way to the airport. Plenty of time. Ithiel drove very slowly. The next shuttle flight wouldn't be taking off until nine o'clock. Clara was glad they didn't have to rush.

"You don't mind my wearing this ring tonight?" said Clara.

"Because this is a bad time to remind me of the way it might have gone with us? No. You came down to see how I was and what you could do for me."

"Next time, Ithiel, if there is a next time, you'll let me check the woman out. You may be big in political analysis . . . No need to finish *that* sentence. Besides, my own judgment hasn't been one hundred percent."

"If anybody were to ask me, Clara, I'd say that you were a strange case—a woman who hasn't been corrupted, who developed her own moral logic, worked it out independently by her own solar power and from her own feminine premises. You hear I've had a calamity and you come down on the next shuttle. And how few people take this Washington flight for a human purpose. Most everybody comes on business. Some to see the sights, a few because of the pictures at the National Gallery, a good percentage to get laid. How many come because they're deep?"

He parked his car so that he could walk with her to the gate.

"You're a dear man," she said. "We have to look out for each other."

On the plane, she pulled her seat belt tight in order to control her feelings, and she opened a copy of *Vogue*, but only to keep her face in it. No magazine now had anything to tell her.

When she got back to Park Avenue, the superintendent's wife, a Latino lady, was waiting. Mrs. Peralta was there too. Clara had asked the cleaning lady to help Gina entertain (to keep an eye on) her friends. The elevator operator–doorman was with the ladies, a small group under the marquee. The sidewalks of Park Avenue are twice as broad as any others, and the median strip was nicely planted with flowers of the season. When the doorman helped Clara from the yellow cab, the women immediately began to tell her about the huge bash Gina had given. "A real mix of people," said Mrs. Peralta.

"And the girls?"

"Oh, we were careful with them, kept them away from those East Harlem types. We're here because Mr. Regler called to say what flight you'd be on."

"I asked him to do that," said Clara.

"I don't think Gina thought so many were coming. Friends, and friends of friends, of her boyfriend, I guess."

"Boyfriend? Now, who would he be? This is news to me."

"I asked Marta Elvia to come and see for herself," said Antonia Peralta. Marta Elvia, the super's wife, was related somehow to Antonia.

They were taken up in the elevator. Marta Elvia, eight months pregnant and filling up much of the space, was saying what a grungy mob had turned up. It was an open house.

"But tell me, quickly, who is the boyfriend?" said Clara.

The man was described as coming from the West Indies; he was French-speaking, dark-skinned, very good-looking, "arrogant like," said Mrs. Peralta.

"And how long has he been coming to the house?"

"Couple of weeks, just."

When she entered the living room, Clara's first impression was: So this is what can be done here. It doesn't have to be the use I put it to. She had limited the drawing room to polite behavior.

The party was mostly over; there were only four or five couples left. As Clara described it, the young women looked gaudy. "The room was more like a car of the West Side subway. Lots of muscle on the boys, as if they did aerobics. And I used to be able to identify the smell of pot, but I'm in the dark, totally, on the new drugs. Crack is completely beyond me; I can't even say what it is, much less describe how it works and does it have a smell. The whole scene was like a mirage to me, how they were haberdashed. Gina's special friend, Frederic, was a good-looking boy, black, and he did have an attractive French accent. Gina tried to behave as if nothing at all was wrong, and she couldn't quite swing that. I wasn't going to fuss at her, though. At the back of the apartment, I had three children sleeping. At a time like this your history books come back to you—how a pioneer woman dealt with an Indian war party when her husband was away. So I put myself out to make time pass pleasantly, toned down the music, ventilated the smoke, and soon the party petered out."

While Mrs. Peralta was cleaning up, Clara had a talk with Gina Wegman. She said she had imagined a smaller gathering—a few acquaintances, not a random sample of the street population.

"Frederic asked if he could bring some friends."

Well, Clara was willing to believe that this was simply a European misconception of partying in New York—carefree musical young people, racially mixed, dancing to reggae music. In Vienna, as elsewhere, such pictures of American life were on TV—America as the place where you let yourself go.

"Anyway, I must tell you, Gina, that I can't allow this kind of thing—like scenes from some lewd dance movie."

"I'm sorry, Mrs. Velde."

"Where did you meet Frederic?"

"Through friends from Austria. They work at the UN."

"Is that where he works too?"

"I never asked."

"And do you see a lot of him? You don't have to answer—I can tell you're taken with him. You never asked what he does? He's not a student?"

"It never came up."

Clara thought, judging by Gina's looks, that what came up was Gina's skirt. Clara herself knew all too well how that was. We've been through it. What can be more natural in a foreign place than to accept exotic experiences? Otherwise why leave home at all?

Clifford, a convict in Attica, still sent Clara a Christmas card without fail. She hadn't seen him in twenty-five years. They had no other connection. Frederic, to go by appearances, wouldn't even have sent a card. Generational differences. Clifford had been a country boy.

We must see to it that it doesn't end badly, was what Clara told herself.

But then we must learn what sort of person Gina is, really, she thought. What makes her tick, and if this is the whole sum of what she wants. I didn't take her for a little hot-pants type.

"I suppose things are done differently in Vienna," Clara said. "As to bringing strangers into the house . . ."

"No. But then you're personally friendly with the colored lady who works here."

"Mrs. Peralta is no stranger."

"She brings her children here at Thanksgiving, and they eat with the girls at the same table."

"And why not? But yes," said Clara, "I can see that this is a mixture that might puzzle somebody just over from Europe for the first time. My husband and I are not rashists. . . ." (This was a pronunciation Clara could not alter.) "However, Mrs. Peralta is a trusted member of this household."

"But Frederic's friends might steal . . . ?"

"I haven't accused anyone. You couldn't vouch for anybody, though. You've just met these guests yourself. And haven't you noticed the security arrangements—the doors, the buzzer system, everybody inspected?"

Gina said, speaking quietly and low, "I noticed. I didn't apply it to myself."

Not *herself*. Gina hadn't considered Frederic in this light. And she couldn't allow him to be viewed with suspicion. Clara gave her a good mark for loyalty. Ten on a scale of ten, she thought, and warmed toward Gina. "It's not a color question. The corporation I'm in has even divested itself in South Africa." This was not a strong statement. To Clara, South Africa was about as close as Xanadu. But she said to herself that they were being diverted into absurdities, and what she and Gina were telling each other was only so much fluff. The girl had come to New York to learn about such guys as Frederic, and there wasn't all that much to learn. This was simply an incident, and not even a good incident. Just a lot of exciting trouble. Then she made a mental note to take all this up with Ithiel and also get his opinion on divestiture.

"Well," she said, "I'm afraid I'm going to set a limit on the size of the group you can entertain."

The girl nodded. That made sense. She couldn't deny it.

No more scolding. And a blend of firmness and concern for the girl. If she were to send her away, the kids would cry. And I'd miss her myself, Clara admitted. So she stood up (mistress terminating a painful interview was how Clara perceived it; she saw that she really had come to depend on certain lady-of-the-house postures). When Gina had gone to her room, Clara ran a check: the Jensen ashtray, the silver letter opener, mantelpiece knick-knacks; and for the nth time she wished that there were someone to share her burdens. Wilder was no good to her that way. If he got fifty speech commissions he couldn't make up the money he had sunk in mining stocks—Homestake and Sunshine. Supposedly, precious metals were a hedge, but there was less and less principal for the shrinking hedge to hedge.

The inspection over, Clara talked to Antonia Peralta before Antonia turned on the noisy vacuum cleaner. How often had Gina's young man been in the apartment? Antonia jabbed at her cheek with a rigid finger, meaning that a sharp lookout was necessary. Her message was: "Count on me, Mrs. Velde." Well, she was part of a pretty smart subculture. Between them, she and Marta Elvia would police the joint. On Gina Wegman herself Antonia Peralta did not comment. But then she wasn't always around, she had her days off. And remember, Antonia hadn't cleaned under the bed. And if she *had* been thorough she would have found the missing ring. In that case, would she have handed it over? She was an honest lady, according to her lights, but there probably were certain corners into which those lights never were turned. The insurance company had paid up, and Clara would have been none the wiser if Antonia had silently pocketed a lost object. No, the Spanish ladies were honest enough. Marta Elvia was bonded, triple certified, and Antonia Peralta had never taken so much as a handkerchief.

"In my own house," Clara was to explain later, "I object to locking up valuables. A house where there is no basic trust is not what I call a house. I just can't live with a bunch of keys, like a French or Italian person. Women have told me that they couldn't sleep nights if their jewelry weren't locked up. *I* couldn't sleep if it were."

She said to Gina, "I'm taking your word for it that nothing bad will happen." She was bound to make this clear, while recognizing that there was no way to avoid giving offense.

Gina had no high looks, no sharp manner. She simply said, "Are you telling me not to have Frederic here?"

Clara's reaction was, Better here than *there*. She tried to imagine what Frederic's pad must be like. That was not too difficult. She had, after all, herself been a young woman in New York. Gina was giving her a foretaste of what she would have to face when her own girls grew up. Unless heaven itself were to decree that Gogmagogsville had gone far enough, and checked the decline—time to lower the boom, send in the Atlantic to wash it away. Not a possibility you could count on.

"By no means," said Clara. "I will ask you, though, to take full charge when Antonia is off."

"You don't want Frederic here when the children are with me?"

"Right."

"He wouldn't harm them."

Clara did not see fit to say more.

She spoke to Ms. Wong about it, stopping at her place after work for a brief drink, a breather on the way home. Ms. Wong had an unsuitably furnished Madison Avenue apartment, Scandinavian design, not an Oriental touch about it except some Chinese prints framed in blond wood. Holding her iced Scotch in a dampening paper napkin, Clara said, "I hate to be the one enforcing the rules on that girl. I feel for her a lot more than I care to."

"You identify all that much with her?"

"She's got to learn, of course," said Clara. "Just as I did. And I don't think much of mature women who have evaded it. But sometimes the schooling we have to undergo is too rough."

"Seems to you *now* . . ."

"No, it takes far too much out of a young girl."

"You're thinking of three daughters," said Ms. Wong, accurate enough.

"I'm thinking how it is that you have to go on for twenty years before you understand—maybe understand—what there was to preserve."

Somewhat dissatisfied with her visit to Laura (it was so *New York!*), she walked home, there to be told by Mrs. Peralta that she had found Gina and Frederic stretched out on the living room sofa. Doing what? Oh, only petting, but the young man with the silk pillows under his combat boots. Clara could see why Antonia should be offended. The young man was putting down the Veldes and their fine upholstery, spreading himself about and being arrogant. And perhaps it wasn't even that. He may not have reached *that* level of intentional offensiveness.

"You talk to the girl?"

"I don't believe I will. No," said Clara, and risked being a contemptible American in Mrs. Peralta's eyes, one of those people who let themselves be run over in their own homes. Largely to herself, Clara explained, "I'd rather put up with him here than have the girl do it in his pad." No sooner had she said this than she was dead certain that there was nothing to keep Gina from doing whatever they did in both places. She would have said to Gina, "Making the most of New York—this not-for-Vienna behavior. No boys lying on top of you in your mother's drawing room." "Land of opportunity," she might have said, but she said this only to herself after thinking matters through, considering deeply in a trance-like private stillness and moistening the center of her upper lip with the tip of her tongue. Why did it go so dry right at the center? Imagining sexual things some-times did that to her. She didn't envy Gina; the woman who had made such personal sexual disclosures to Ms. Wong didn't have to envy anyone. No, she was curious about this pretty, plump girl. She sensed that she was a deep one. *How* deep was what Clara was trying to guess when she went so still.

And so she closed her eyes briefly, nodding, when Marta Elvia, who sometimes waited for her in the lobby, pressed close with her pregnant belly to say that Frederic had come in at one o'clock and left just before Mrs. Velde was expected.

(There were anomalies in Clara's face when you saw it frontally. Viewing it in profile, you would find yourself trying to decide which of the Flemish masters would have painted her best.)

"Thanks, Marta Elvia," she said. "I've got the situation under control."

She shouldn't have been so sure about it, for that very evening when she was dressing for dinner—a formal cor-porate once-a-year affair—she was standing before the long mirror in her room, when suddenly she knew that her ring had been stolen. She kept it in the top drawer of her dresser—unlocked, of course. Its place was a dish Jean-Claude had given her years ago. The young Frenchman, Ithiel's temporary replacement recklessly chosen in anger, had called this gift a *vide-poches*. At bedtime you emptied your pockets into it. It was meant for men; women didn't use that kind of object; but it was one of those mementos Clara couldn't part with—she kept schoolday valentines in a box, too. She looked, of course, into the dish. The ring wasn't there. She hadn't expected it to be. She expected nothing. She said that the sudden knowledge that it was gone came over her like death and she felt as if the life had been vacuumed out of her.

Wilder, already in evening clothes, was reading one of his thrillers in a corner where the back end of the grand piano hid him. With her rapid, dry decisionmaker's look, Clara went to the kitchen, where the kids were at dinner. Under Gina's influence they behaved so well at table. "May I see you for a moment?" said Clara, and Gina immediately got up and followed her to the master bedroom. There Clara shut both doors, and lowering her head so that she seemed to be examining Gina's eyes, "Well, Gina, something has happened," she said. "My ring is gone."

"You mean the emerald that was lost and found again? Oh, Mrs. Velde, I am sorry. Is it gone? I'm sure you have looked. Did Mr. Velde help you?"

"I haven't told him yet."

"Then let's look together."

"Yes, let's. But it's always in the same place, in this room. In that top drawer under my stockings. Since I found it again, I've been extra careful. And of course I want to examine the shag rug. I want to crawl and hunt for it. But I'd have to take off this tight dress to get on my knees. And my hair is fixed for going out."

Gina, stooping, combed through the carpet near the dresser. Clara, silent, let her look, staring down, her eyes superdilated, her mouth stern. She said, at last, "It's no use." She had let Gina go through the motions.

"Should you call the police to report it?"

"I'm not going to do that," said Clara. She was not so foolish as to tell the young woman about the insurance. "Perhaps that makes you feel better, not having the police."

"I think, Mrs. Velde, you should have locked up your valuable objects."

"In my own home, I shouldn't have to."

"Yes, but there are other people also to consider."

"I consider, Gina, that a woman has a right in her own bedroom . . . it's for a woman *herself* to decide who comes in. I made it explicit what the household rules were. I would have vouched for you, and you must vouch for your friend."

Gina was shaken. Both women trembled. After all, thought Clara, a human being can be sketched in three or four lines, but then when the sockets are empty, no amount of ingenuity can refill them. Not her brown, not my blue.

"I understand you," said Gina with an air of being humiliated by a woman whose kindness she counted on. "Are you sure the ring isn't misplaced again?"

"Are *you* sure . . . ?" Clara answered. "And try to think of my side of it. That was an engagement ring from a man who loved me. It's not just an object worth X dollars. It's also a life support, my dear." She was about to say that it was involved with her very grip on existence, but she didn't want any kind of cry to come out or to betray a fear of total slippage. She said instead, "The ring was here yesterday. And a person I don't know wandering around the house and—why not?—coming into my room . . ."

"Why don't you say it?" said Gina.

"I'd have to be a fool not to. To be too nice for such things, I'd have to be a moron. Frederic was here all afternoon. Has he got a job somewhere?"

The girl had no answer to this.

"You can't say. But you don't believe he's a thief. You don't think he'd put you in this position. And don't try to tell me he's being accused because of his color."

"I didn't try. People *are* nasty about the Haitians."

"You'd better go and talk to him. If he's got the ring, tell him he has to return it. I want you to produce it tomorrow. Marta Elvia can sit with the girls if you have to go out tonight. Where does he live?"

"One hundred twenty-eighth Street."

"And a telephone? You can't go up there alone after

dark. Not even by day. Not alone. And where does he
hang out? I can ask Antonia's husband to take you by
cab. . . . Now Wilder's coming down the corridor, and
I've got to go."

"I'll wait here for the concierge."

"For Marta Elvia. I'll talk to her on the way out. *You*
wouldn't steal, Gina. And Mrs. Peralta has been here
eight years without a coffee spoon missing."

Later Clara took it out on herself: What did I do to
that girl, like ordering her to go to Harlem, where she
could be raped or killed, because of my goddam ring,
the rottenest part of town in the rotten middle of the
night, frantic mad and (what it comes down to) over
Ithiel, who balked at marrying me twenty years ago! A
real person understands how to cut losses, not let her
whole life be wound around to the end by a single desire,
because under it all is the uglitude of this one hang-up.
Four husbands and three kids haven't cured me of Ithiel.
And finally this love-toy emerald, personal sentimental-
ity, makes me turn like a maniac on this Austrian kid.
She may think I grudge her the excitement of her romance with that disgusting girl-fucker who used her as
his cover to get into the house and now sticks her with
this theft.

Nevertheless Clara had fixed convictions about do-
mestic and maternal responsibilities. She had already
gone too far in letting Gina bring Frederic into the apartment and infect the whole place, spraying it with sexual
excitement. And, as it now turned out, even become in-

volved in crime. A fling in the U.S.A. was all very well for a young lady from bourgeois Vienna—like the poor Russian hippie, that diplomat's son who fell in love with Mick Jagger. "Tell Mick Jagger goodbye," he said, boarding the plane. This city had become the center, the symbol of worldwide adolescent revolt.

In the middle of the corporate evening Clara was attacked by one of her fierce migraines, and a head as conspicuous as hers, dominating a dinner table, affected everybody when it began to ache, so that the whole party stood up when she rose and hurried out. The Veldes went straight home. Swallowing a handful of white pills from the medicine chest, Clara went immediately to Gina's room. To her relief, the girl was there, in bed. The reading lamp was on, but she wasn't reading, only sitting up, her hands thoughtfully folded.

"I'm glad you didn't go to Harlem!"

"I reached Frederic on the phone. He was with some of our UN friends."

"And you'll see him tomorrow . . . ?"

"I didn't mention the ring. But I am prepared to move out. You told me I had to bring it back or leave."

"Going where . . . !" Clara was taken by surprise. Next she was aware of the girl's brown gaze, the exceptional fixity of it. Unshed tears were killing her. "But if Frederic gives back the ring, you'll stay." While she was speaking, Clara with some shame recognized how dumb she sounded. It was the hereditary peasant in her saying this. The guy would deny the theft, and if eventually he admitted it, he still would not return the ring. This very moment he might be taking a thousand bucks for it. These people came up from the tropical slums to outsmart New York, and with all the rules crumbling here as elsewhere, so that nobody could any longer be clear in his mind about anything, they could do it.

Left standing were only property rights. With murder in second place. A stolen ring. A corpse to account for. Such were the only universals recognized, and very few others could be acknowledged. So where did love fit in? Love was down in the catacombs, those catacombs being the personal neuroses of women like herself.

She said to Gina, as one crypto lover to another, "What will you do?"

Gina said, but without resentment, not a hint of accusation in her voice, "That I can't say. I've only had a couple of hours to think. There are places."

She'd move in with her Haitian, Clara guessed, plausibly enough. But this was not sayable. Clara was learning to refrain. You didn't *say* everything. "Discover silence," she instructed herself.

Next day she rushed home from work in a cab and found Marta Elvia baby-sitting. Clara had already been in touch with an agency, and there was a new girl coming tomorrow. Best she could do on short notice. Lucy was upset, predictably, and Clara had to take her aside for special explanations. She said, "Gina suddenly had to go. It was an emergency. She didn't *want* to. When she can, she'll come back. It's not *your* fault." There was no guessing just how rattled Lucy was. She was silent, stoical.

Clara had rehearsed this on the telephone with the psychiatrist, Dr. Gladstone.

"With working parents," she said to Lucy, "such problems do come up."

"But Daddy isn't working now."

You're telling *me*! thought Clara. He was doping out the upcoming primaries in New Hampshire.

As soon as possible, she went to see Dr. Gladstone. He was about to take one of his holidays and would be away three weeks. They had discussed this absence in the last session. In the waiting room, she studied the notes she had prepared: Where is Gina? How can I find out, keep track? Protect?

She acknowledged to Dr. Gladstone that she was in a near-hysterical state over the second disappearance, the theft. She was discovering that she had come to base her stability entirely on the ring. Such dependency was fearful. He asked how she saw this, and how Ithiel figured in it. She said, "The men I meet don't seem to be real persons. Nobody really is anybody. There may be more somebodies than I've been able to see. I don't want to write off about one half of our species. And concentrated desire for so many years may have affected my judgment. Anyway, for me, what a man is seems to be defined by

Ithiel. Also, I am *his* truest friend, and he understands that and responds emotionally."

Involuntarily Clara fell into Dr. Gladstone's way of talking. To herself, she would never say "responds emotionally." As the sessions were short, she adopted his lingo to save time, notwithstanding the danger of false statements. Hope brought her here, every effort must be made, but when she looked, looked with all her might at Dr. Gladstone, she could not justify the trust she was asked to place in that samurai beard, the bared teeth it framed, the big fashionable specs, his often baseless confidence in his science. However, it would take the better part of a year to acquaint a new doctor with the fundamentals of her case. She was stuck with this one.

"And I'm very worried about Gina. How do I find out what's happening to her? Should I hire a private investigator? A girl like that survive in Spanish Harlem? No way."

"An expensive proposition," said Dr. Gladstone. "Any alternatives in mind?"

"Wilder does nothing. *He* could get on the case. Like shadow her, make practical use of the thrillers he's read. But he's negotiating with some hopeless wimp who wants to go for the White House."

"Let's get back to the theft, if it *is* a theft."

"It *has* to be. I didn't misplace it again."

"However, it gave you daily anxiety. Why did it occupy so big a place in you?"

"What did I come up with last time we discussed it? I cheated the insurance company and had the ring *and* the money. You could call that white-collar crime. It all added to the importance of my emerald, but I would never have guessed that it would be so shattering to lose it."

"I can suggest a coincidence," said the doctor. "At this bad moment for you I am going on a holiday. My support is removed. And my name is Glad*stone*. Is that why you take the loss so hard?"

Astonished, she gave him a real stare, not a fitting or becoming one. She said, "You may be a stone, but you're not a gem."

When she returned to her office she telephoned Ithiel, her only dependable adviser, to discuss matters.

"I wish you were coming up to New York," she said. "I used to call on Steinsalz when things were urgent."

"He was a great loss to me too."

"He took such interest in people. Short of lending them money. He'd treat you to dinner but never lend a cent. He did listen, though."

"It so happens," said Ithiel (when he was being methodical, a sort of broken flatness entered his voice), "that I have a lunch date next Tuesday with a man in New York."

"Let's say half-past three, then?"

Their customary meeting place was St. Patrick's cathedral, near Clara's office, a central location and a shelter in bad weather. "Like a drop for secret agents," Ithiel said. They left the cathedral and went directly to the Helmsley Palace. A quiet corner of the bar was still available at that early hour. "This is on my Gold Card," said Clara. "Now let's see how you look—somewhere between a Spanish grandee and a Mennonite."

Then with executive rapidity she set forth the main facts.

"What's your opinion of Frederic—an occasional stealer or a pro?"

"I think he improvises," said Clara. "Dope? Probably."

"You could find out about his police record, if any. Then ask the Austrian consulate about her. Not telephone her folks in Vienna."

"I knew it would be a relief to talk to you. Now tell me . . . about the ring."

"A loss, I'd guess. Write it off."

"I suppose I'll have to. I indulged myself about it, and look at the trouble it made. There's nothing appropriate. For instance, this luxury bar that fits neither you nor me. In my true feelings you and I are as naked as Adam and Eve. I'm not being suggestive, either. It's not an erotic suggestion, just a simile."

Talk like this, the hint of wildness in it, had the effect of forcing him into earnestness. She could see him applying his good mind to her difficulties, like a person outside pressing his forehead on the windowpane to see what's going on.

As she figured it, he counted on the executive Clara to gain on the subjective Clara. She *did* have the ability to put her house in order. Yet his sympathy for the subjective, personal Clara was very strong. Considering the greater tumult in her, she had done better than he. Even now her life was more coherent than his.

"For a few hundred bucks, I think you can find out where the girl is. Investigators are easy to hire."

"Tell me! I can see why General Haig and such people call on you to analyze the Iranians or the Russians. By the way, Wilder thought you were great on TV with Dobrynin, week before last."

When Ithiel smiled, his teeth were so good you suspected Hollywood dentistry, but they were all his own.

"Dobrynin has some genius, of a low kind. He convinces Americans that Russians are exactly like them. Sometimes he behaves as if he were the senior senator from a fifty-first, all-Russian state. Just a slight accent, but the guys from the Deep South have one also. He sold Gorbachev on this completely, and Gorbachev is selling the whole U.S.A. Which craves to be sold. Deceived, if you prefer."

"Like me, in a way, about the Human Pair."

"You're close to that girl, I see."

"Very close. It would be easy for you to put her down as a well-brought-up kid with a taste for low sex. Resembling me. You'd be wrong. Too bad you can't see her yourself. Your opinion would interest me."

"So she isn't like you?"

"I sure hope not." Clara made a gesture, as if saying, Wipe out these Helmsley Palace surroundings and listen to me. "Don't forget my two suicide attempts. I have a spoonful of something wild in my mixture, my whole sense of . . ."

"Of life . . ."

"Listen to me. You have no idea really how wild and how mixed, or how much territory it takes in. The territory stretches over into death. When I'm drunk with agitation—and it is like being drunk—there's one pulse in me that's a death-beat pulse, and it tempts me to make out with death. It says, Why wait! When I get as intense as that, existence won't hold me. That's the internal horror side of the thing. I'm open to seduction by death. Now you're going to remind me that I'm the mother of three kids."

"Exactly what I was about to do."

"There's no one in the world but you that I'd say this to. You're the one human being I fully confide in. Neither do you have secrets from me. Whatever you didn't admit I saw for myself."

"You certainly did, Clara."

"But we'll never be man and wife. Oh, you don't have to say anything. You love me, but the rest is counter-indicated. It's one of those damn paradoxes that have to be waited out. There may even be a parallel to it in your field, in politics. We have the power to destroy ourselves, and maybe the desire, and we keep ourselves in permanent suspense—waiting. Isn't that wild, too? You could tell *me*. You're the expert. You're going to write the book of books about it."

"Now you're making fun of me."

"Not really, Ithiel. If it is the book of books on the subject, it should be written. You may be the man to write it, and I'm not making fun. For *me* it would be funny. Think of a great odalisque, nude and beautiful. And now think of her in eyeglasses and writing books on a lap board."

Over the table they smiled briefly at each other.

"But I want to get back to Gina," said Clara. "You're going to find me a dependable investigator to check out Frederic, and the rest of it. I doubt that she is like me, except in taking chances. But when I told her that the ring was given by a man who loved me, the fact registered completely. What I didn't add was that I bullied you into giving it to me. Don't deny it. I twisted your arm. Then I sentimentalized it. Then I figured out that you continued to love me *because* we didn't marry. And now the ring . . . The girl understands about the ring. The love part of it."

Teddy was stirred, and looked aside. He wasn't ready, and perhaps never would be ready, to go farther. No, they never would be man and wife. When they stood up to go, they kissed like friends.

"You'll get me an investigator with a little class . . . the minimum sleaze?"

"I'll tell the man to go to your office, so you can look him over."

"A few things have to be done for you too," said Clara.

"That Francine left you in bad shape. You have that somber look that you get when you're up against it."

"Is that what you mean by the Mennonite?"

"There were plenty of Mennonites in Indiana—I can tell that you didn't have any business in New York today except me."

Within ten days she had Gina's address—a fourth-floor walk-up on East 128th Street, care of F. Vigneron. She had a phone number as well. Call? No, she wouldn't speak to her yet. She brought her executive judgment to bear on this, and the advice from this source was to send a note. In her note, she wrote that the children asked for Gina often. Lucy missed her. Even so, she had done Lucy good. You could see the improvements. There was a lot of woman in that small girl, already visible. Then, speaking for herself, she said that she was sorry to have come down so hard on a matter that needn't be spelled out now. She had left Gina few options. She had had no choice but to go. The mystery was why she had gone "uptown" when other choices were possible. However, Gina owed her no explanations. And Clara hoped that she would not feel that she had to turn away from her forever or decide that she, Clara, was an enemy. Anything but a hostile judge, Clara respected her sense of honor.

Asked for a reference on her unlisted mental line,

Clara, when reached, would have said about Gina: soft face, soft bust, brown bourgeois-maiden gaze, but firm at decision time. Absolutely ten on a scale of ten.

But in the note she sent to Gina she went on, ladylike, matronly and fair-minded, to wish her well, and concluded, "You should have had some notice, and I believe it only fair that the month should have been rounded out, so since I am not absolutely certain of the correct address, I will leave an envelope with Marta Elvia. Two hundred dollars in cash."

Frederic Vigneron would send her for the money, if he got wind of it.

Gottschalk, the private eye, did his job responsibly; that was about the best that could be said of him. Perhaps half an eye. And not much more ear. Still, he did obtain the facts she asked for. He said of the building in East Harlem, "Of course the city can't run around and condemn every joint it should, or there'd be lots more street people sleeping in the West Side terminal. But I wouldn't want any nieces of mine living there."

Having done what you could, you went ahead with your life: showered and powdered with talcum in the morning, put on underthings and stockings, chose a skirt and blouse for the day, made up your face for the office, took in the paper, and, if Wilder was sleeping in (he did often), ground your coffee and as the water dripped turned the pages of the *Times* professionally. For a group of magazines owned by a publishing corporation, she was the lady overseeing women's matters. Almost too influential to have a personal life, as she sometimes observed to Ms. Wong. High enough in the power structure, you can be excused from having one, "an option lots of people are glad to exercise."

Nobody called for the money envelope. Marta Elvia's instructions were to give it to Gina only. After a period of keen interest, Clara stopped asking about it. Gottschalk, doing little, sent an occasional memo: "Status quo unchanged." To go with his Latin, Clara figured that Gina had found a modus vivendi with her young Haitian. The weeks, week after week, subdued Clara. You can say that you're waiting only if there is something definite to wait for. During this time it often seemed there wasn't anything. And, "I never feel so bad as when the life I lead stops being characteristic—when it could be anybody else's life," she told Laura Wong.

But coming home one afternoon after a session with Dr. Gladstone (things were so bad that she was seeing him regularly again), she entered her bedroom for an hour's rest before the kids returned from ballet class. She had dropped her shoes and was crawling toward the pillows, her mouth open in the blindness of fatigue, surrendering to the worst of feelings, when she saw that her ring had been placed on the night table. It had been set on a handkerchief, a new object from a good shop. She slipped on her ring and lunged for the phone across the bed, rapidly punching out Marta Elvia's number.

"Marta Elvia," she said, "has anybody been here today? Did anybody come to leave an article for me?" Fifteen years in the U.S. and the woman still spoke incomplete English. "Listen," said Clara. "Did Gina come here today? Did you or anybody let Gina into the apartment? . . . No? Somebody did come in, and Gina gave up her house keys when she left. . . . Sure she could have made a duplicate—she or her boyfriend. . . . Of course I should have changed the lock. . . . No, nothing was taken. On the contrary, the person gave back something. I'm glad I didn't change the lock."

Now Marta Elvia was upset that an outside somebody had got in. Security in this building was one hundred percent. She was sending her husband up to make sure the door hadn't been jimmied open.

"No, no!" said Clara. "There hasn't been illegal entry. What a wild idea!"

Her own ideas at this moment were not less wild. She rang Gina's number in East Harlem. What she got was an answering machine, from which came Frederic's voice, whose Frenchy slickness was offensive. (Clara disliked those telephone devices anyway, and her prejudice extended to the sound of the signal—in this instance a pig squeal.) "This is Mrs. Wilder Velde calling Miss Wegman." Inasmuch as Gina might have prevailed by reasonable means over him, Clara was ready to revise her opinion of Frederic too. (On her scale of ten, she could upgrade him from less than zero to one.)

Next Clara phoned Gottschalk and entered on his tape her request that he call back. She then tried Laura Wong, and finally Wilder in New Hampshire. It was primary time up there; his candidate lagged far behind the field, and you couldn't expect Wilder to be in his hotel room. Ithiel was in Central America. There was no one to share the recovery of the ring with. The strongest lights in the house were in the bathroom, and she turned them on, pressing against the sink to examine the stone and the setting, making sure that the small diamonds were all there. Since Mrs. Peralta had been in that day, she tried her number—she had a crying need to talk with somebody—and this time actually succeeded. "Did anybody come into the house today?"

"Only deliveries, by the service elevator."

During this unsatisfactory conversation Clara had a view of herself in the hall mirror—a bony woman, not young, blond but not fair, gaunt, a long face, a hollow cheek, not rejoicing, and pressing the ringed hand under the arm that held the phone. The big eyes ached, and looked it. Feeling so high, why did she appear so low? But did she think that recovering the ring would make her young?

What she believed—and it was more than a belief; there was triumph in it—was that Gina Wegman had come into the bedroom and placed the ring on the nightstand.

And how had Gina obtained the ring, what had she had to promise, or sacrifice, or pay? Maybe her parents had wired money from Vienna. Suppose that her only purpose during four months had been nothing but restitution, and that the girl had done her time in East Harlem for no other reason? It struck Clara that if Gina had stolen the emerald back from Frederic and run away, then leaving a message on his machine had been a bad mistake. He might put it all together and come after Gina with a gun. There was even a private eye in this quickly fermenting plot. Except that Gottschalk was no Philip Marlowe in a Raymond Chandler story. Nevertheless he was a detective of some kind. He must be licensed to carry a gun. And everybody's mind ran in these psychopathic-melodrama channels streaming with blood, or children's fingerpaints, or blood that naive people took for fingerpaint. The fancy (or hope) that Gottschalk would kill Frederic in a shoot-out was so preposterous that it helped Clara to calm herself.

When she received Gottschalk in her office next day, she was wearing the ring and showed it to him. He said, "That's a high-value object. I hope you don't take public transportation to work." She looked disdainful. There was a livery service. He didn't seem to realize how high her executive bracket was. But he said, "There are people in top positions who insist on using the subway. I could name you a Wall Street woman who goes to work disguised as a bag lady so it isn't worthwhile to hassle her."

"I believe Gina Wegman entered my apartment yesterday and left the emerald by my bed."

"Must've been her."

Gottschalk's personal observation was that Mrs. Velde hadn't slept last night.

"It couldn't have been the *man*," she said. "What's your professional conclusion about him?"

"Casual criminal. Not enough muscle for street crime."

"She didn't marry him, did she?"

"I could run a check on that. My guess is no."

"What you can find out for me is whether she's still on One hundred twenty-eighth Street. If she grabbed the ring and brought it back, he may do her some harm."

"Well, ma'am, he's been in the slammer a few times for petty stuff. He wouldn't do anything major." Frederic had been one of those boat people lucky enough to reach Florida a few years back. So much Clara knew.

"After stealing your ring, he didn't even know how to fence it."

Clara said, "I have to find out where she's living. I have to see the girl. Get hold of her. I'll pay a bonus— within reason."

"Send her to your house?"

"That might embarrass her—the girls, Mrs. Peralta, my husband. Say I want to have lunch with her. Ask her whether she received my note."

"Let me look into it."

"Quickly. I don't want this dragging on."

"Top priority," said Gottschalk.

She counted on the suite of offices to impress him, and she was glad now that she had paid his bills promptly.

Keeping on his good side, taking care from every stand-point to be a desirable client. As for Gottschalk, he was exactly what she had ordered from Ithiel—minimum sleaze. Not much more.

"I'd like a progress report by Friday," she said.

That afternoon she met with Ms. Wong. Moved to talk. And with the gesture of a woman newly engaged, she held out her hand, saying, "Here's the ring. I thought it had gone into the muck for good. It's getting to be a fairy-tale object. With me it's had the funny effect of those trick films they used to show kids—first a building demol-ished by dynamite. They show it coming down. Then they reverse it in slow motion, and it's put together again."

"Done by means of a magic ring?" said Ms. Wong.

It occurred to Clara that Laura was a mysterious lady too. She was exotic in externals, but in what she said she was perfectly conventional. While your heart was moved; she would still murmur along. If you came and told her you were going to kill yourself, what would she do? Prob-ably nothing. Yet one must talk.

"I can't say what state I'm in," said Clara, "whether I'm pre-dynamite or post-dynamite. I don't suppose I look demolished. . . ."

"Certainly not."

"Yet I feel as if something had come down. There are changes. Gina, for instance, was a girl I took into the house to help with the kids. Little was ever said. I didn't think well of her Caribbean romance, or sex experiment.

Just another case of being at sea amongst collapsing cultures—I sound like Ithiel now, and I don't actually take much stock in the collapsing-culture bit: I'm beginning to see it instead as the conduct of life without input from your soul. Essential parts of people getting mislaid or crowded out—don't ask me for specifics; I can't give them. They're always flitting by me. But what I started to say was how I've come to love that girl. Just as she immediately understood Lucy, how needy Lucy was, in one minute she also got the whole meaning of this ring. And on the decision to get it back for me she left the house. Moving to East Harlem, yet."

"If her Vienna family had a notion . . ."

"I intend to do something for her. That's a special young woman. I certainly will do something. I have to think what it should be. Now, I don't expect her to describe what she went through, and I don't intend to ask her. There are things I wouldn't want anybody to ask me," said Clara. Clifford from Attica was on her mind. On the whole, she kept this deliberately remote, yet if pressed she could recover quite a lot from her memory.

"Have you any idea . . . ?" said Laura Wong.

"About her, not yet, not until I've spoken to her. About myself, however, I do have different views as a result of this. Twice losing and recovering this ring is a sign, a message. It forces me to interpret. For instance, when Francine came in a van and emptied Ithiel's house—that woman is about as human as a toilet plunger!—

Ithiel didn't turn to me. He didn't come and say, 'You're unhappy with Wilder. And between us we've had seven marriages. Now, shouldn't you and I . . . ?' "

"Clara, you wouldn't have done that?" said Laura. For once her voice was more real. Clara was struck by the difference.

"I *might* have done it. So far it's been change and change and change. There's pleasure change, and acquisitive change, and there's the dynamic of . . . oh, I don't know. Perhaps of power. Is there no point of rest? Won't the dynamic ever let you go? I felt that Ithiel might be a point of rest. Or I for him. But that was simply goofy. I have an anti-rest character. I think there's too much basic discord in me."

"So the ring stood for hope of Teddy Regler," said Laura Wong.

"The one exception. Teddy. A repeatedly proven exception. There must be others, but I never came across them."

"And do you think . . . ?"

"He'll ever accomplish his aim? I can't say. He can't, either. What he says is that no trained historian will ever do it, only a singular person with a singular eye. Looking at the century with his singular inborn eye, with a genius for observing politics: That's about the way he says it, and perhaps he'll take hold one day and do a wrap-up of the century, the wrap-up of wrap-ups. As for me," said Clara, "I have the kids, with perhaps Wilder thrown in as a fourth child. The last has been unacceptable. What I'd most like now is a quiet life."

"The point of rest?"

"No, I don't expect that. A quiet life in lieu of the point of rest. The point of rest might have been with Ithiel. I have to settle for what I can get—peaceful evenings. Let there be a convent atmosphere, when the kids have gone to bed and I can disconnect the phones and concentrate on Yeats or somebody like that. Not to be too ambitious; it would be enough to get rid of your demons—they're like patients who drift in and out of the mental hospital. In short, come to terms with my anti-rest character."

"So all these years you've never given up hope that Teddy Regler and you . . ."

"Might make a life together, in the end . . . ?" said Clara. Something caused her to hesitate. As they had always done in problematic situations, her eyes turned sideways, looking for an exit, and her country-girl mouth was open but silent.

On Madison Avenue, walking uptown, Clara was thinking, saying to herself in her contralto grumble, This is *totally* off the wall. There's no limit, is there? She wanted me to say that Ithiel and I were finished, so that she could put her own moves on him. Everybody feels free to picture what they like, and I talked Ithiel up until he became too desirable for her to resist, and how long has the little bitch been dreaming of having him for herself! No way! Clara was angry, but she was also laughing about this. So I choose friends, so I choose lovers, so I choose husbands and bankers and accountants and psychiatrists and ministers, all the way down the line. And just now lost my principal confidante. But I have to spin her off very slowly, for if I cut the relationship, she's in a position to hurt me with Wilder. There's also the insurance company, remember, the real owner of this ring. Also, she's so gifted professionally. We still need her layouts.

Meanwhile she had in mind an exceptional, a generous action.

From her office next day, on her private line, she had a preliminary talk about it with Ithiel, just back from Central America. Naturally she couldn't tell him what her goal was. She began by describing the return of her ring, all the strange circumstances. "This very minute, I'm looking at it. Wearing it, I don't feel especially girlish. I'm more like contemplating it."

She could see Ithiel trying on this new development, matching the contemplative Clara against the Clara who had once sunk her long nails into his forearm and left scars that he might have shown General Haig or Henry Kissinger if he had wanted to emphasize a point about violence. He had quite a sense of humor, Ithiel did. He enjoyed telling how, in a men's room at the White House, Mr. Armand Hammer was at the next urinal, and about the discussion on Soviet intentions they had had between the opening and the closing zips.

Or thinking back to the passionate Clara, or to the Clara who had wanted them buried side by side or even in the same grave. This had lately begun to amuse him.

From her New York office, she had continued to talk. So far he had had little to say other than to congratulate her on the recovery of this major symbol, Madison Hamilton's emerald. "This Gina is a special young woman, Ithiel," she told him. "You would have expected such behavior from a Sicilian or a Spanish woman, and not a contemporary, either, but a romantic Stendhal character—a Happy Few type, or a young woman of the Italian Renaissance in one of those Venetian chronicles the Elizabethans took from."

"Not what you would expect from the Vienna of Kurt Waldheim," he said.

"You've got it. And a young person of that quality shouldn't go on tending kids in New York—Gogmagogsville. Now, what I want to suggest is that she go to Washington."

"And you'd like me to find her a job?"

"That wouldn't be easy. She has a student visa, not a green card. I need to get her away from here."

"Save her from the Haitian. I see. However, she may not want to be saved."

"I'll have to find out how she sees it. My hunch is that the Haitian episode is over and she's ready for some higher education. . . ."

"And that's where I come in, isn't it?"

"Don't be light with me about this. I'm asking you to

take me seriously. Remember what you said to me not long ago about my moral logic, worked out on my own feminine premises under my own power. . . . Now, I've never known you to talk through your hat on any real subject."

She had been centered, unified, concentrated, heartened, oriented by his description of her, and she couldn't let him withdraw any part of it.

"What I saw was what I said. Years of observation to back it. Does she want to come to Washington?"

"Well, Ithiel, I haven't had an opportunity to ask her. But . . . so that you'll understand me, I've come to love that girl. I've examined minutely every aspect of what probably happened, and I believe that the man stole the ring because their relationship was coming to an end. Their affair was about over. So he made her an accessory to the theft and she went with him only to get my emerald back."

Ithiel said, "And why do you believe this . . . this scenario of yours—that she was through with him, and he was so cunning, and she had such a great sense of honor, or responsibility? All of it sounds more like *you* than like any sample of the general population."

"But what I'm telling you," she said with special emphasis, "is that Gina isn't a sample from the population, and that I love her."

"And you want us to meet. And she'll come under my influence. She'll fall in love with me. So you and I will increase our number. She'll enlist with us. And she and I will cherish each other, and you will have the comfort of seeing me in safe hands, and this will be your blessing poured over the two of us."

"Teddy, you're making fun of me," she said, but she knew perfectly well that he wasn't making fun, that wasn't where the accent fell, and his interpretation was more or less correct, as far as it went.

"We'll never get each other out of trouble," said Ithiel. "Not the amount of trouble we're in. And even that is not so exceptional. And we all know what to expect. Only a few mavericks fight on. That's you I'm speaking of. I like to think that I'm at home with what is real. Your idea of the real is different. Maybe it's deeper than mine. Now, if your young lady has her own reasons for moving down here to Washington, I'll be happy to meet her for your sake and talk to her. But the sort of arrangements that are ideal for your little children—play school, parties, and concerned teachers—can't be extended to the rest of us."

"Oh, Teddy, I'm not such a fool as you take me for," Clara said.

After this conversation, she drew up a memo pad to try to summarize Ithiel's underlying view: The assumptions we make as to one another's motives are so circumscribed, our understanding of the universe and its forces is so false, that the more we analyze, the more injury we do. She knew perfectly well that this memo, like all the others, would disappear. She'd ask herself, "What was I thinking after my talk with Teddy?" and she'd never see this paper anymore.

Now she had to arrange a meeting with Gina Wegman, and that turned out to be a difficult thing to do. She would never have anticipated that it would be so hard. She repeatedly called Gottschalk, who said he was in touch with Gina. He hadn't actually seen her yet. He now had a midtown number for her and occasionally was able to reach her. "Have you said that I'd like a meeting?" said Clara. She thought, It's shame. The poor kid is ashamed.

"She said she was extremely busy, and I believe there's a plan for her to go home."

"To Austria?"

"She speaks English okay, only I'm not getting a clear signal."

Unkindly, Clara muttered that if he'd keep his glasses clean he'd see more. Also, to increase his importance and his fees, he was keeping information from her—or pretending that he had more information than he actually did have. "If you'd give me the number, I could try a direct call," she said. "Now, is the young man with her, there in midtown?"

"That wouldn't be my guess. I think she's with friends, relatives, and I think she's going back to Vienna real soon. I'll give you her number, but before you call her, let me have a few hours more to get supplementary information for you."

"Fine," said Clara, and as soon as Gottschalk was off the line she dialed Gina. She reached her at once. As simple as that.

"Oh, Mrs. Velde. I meant to call you," said Gina. "I was a little put off by that Mr. Gottschalk. He's a detective, and I worried about your attitude, that you thought it was a police matter."

"He's not police at all, he's strictly private. I needed to find out. I would never have threatened. I wanted to know where you were. The man's a moron. Never mind about him. Is it true, Gina, that you're going to Vienna?"

The young woman said, "Tonight, Lufthansa. Via Munich."

"Without seeing me? Why, that's not possible. I must have made you angry. But it's not anger that I feel toward you; just the opposite. And we have to meet before you leave. You must be rushed with last-minute things." Horrified to be losing her, and dilated with heat and breath, her heart swelling suddenly, she was hardly able to speak because of the emotional stoppage of her throat. "Won't you make some time for me, Gina? There's so much to work out, so much between us. Why the rush home?"

"And I would very much like to see you, Mrs. Velde. The hurry is my engagement and marriage."

Clara wildly guessed, She's pregnant. "Are you marrying Frederic?" she said. It was a charged question, nearly a prayer: Don't let her be as crazy as that. Gina was not prepared to answer. She seemed to be considering. But presently she said, "I wouldn't have to go to

Vienna, in that case. My fiancé is a man from my father's bank."

Whether or not to explain herself must have been the issue. Explanations, in Clara's opinion, should be made. Gina had been wavering, but now she agreed, she decided to see Clara after all. Yes, she was going to do it. "Some friends are giving me a cocktail send-off. That's on Madison in the low Seventies. Maybe half an hour beforehand? . . . In your way, you *were* very kind," Clara heard the girl saying.

"Let's make it at the Westbury, then. When? At four o'clock."

Kind, in my way . . . Signifying what? She feels I was crude. But these side issues could be dealt with later. Right now Clara's appointment with Dr. Gladstone must be canceled. Since the fee would have to be paid notwithstanding, he'd have an hour to think deep analytic thoughts, ponder identity problems, Clara told herself with more than a drop of hatred. Was there anybody who was somebody? How was a man like Gladstone to know! Plumbers was what Ithiel called these Gladstone types. He had quit analysis because nobody was able to tell him what it took to be Ithiel Regler. This sounded haughty, but actually it was the only reasonable thing. It was no more than true. It applied to her as well.

That she should be so firm and assertive was strange, seeing that she was in a fever, trying to regulate an outflow of mingled soiled emotions. In the cab—one of ten thousand cars creeping uptown—she leaned her long neck backward to relieve it of the weight of her head and to control the wildness of her mind, threatened with panic. These gridlocks on Madison Avenue, these absolutely unnecessary mobs, the vehicles that didn't have to be here, carrying idle shoppers or old people with no urgent purpose except to break out of confinement or go and scold someone. Clara was suffocated by this stalling and delay. She exploded engines in her mind, got out at corners and pulled down stoplights with terrible strength. Five of the thirty minutes Gina could give her were already down the drain. Two blocks from the Westbury, she could no longer bear the traffic, and she got out and trotted the rest of the way, the insides of her knees rubbing together as they always did when she was in a rush.

She passed through the four-quartered door into the lobby and there was Gina Wegman just getting up from the tall chair, and how beautiful the girl looked in her round black glossy straw hat with a half veil dropped onto the bridge of her nose. She certainly wasn't gotten up to look contrite, in a dress that showed off her bust and the full lines of her bottom. On the other hand, she wasn't defiant, either. Lively, yes, and brilliant too. She approached Clara with an affectionate gesture so that when they kissed on the cheek Clara captured part of what a passionate man might feel toward a girl like this.

Clara, as she blamed her lateness on the rush hour, was at the same instant dissatisfied with the dress she had put on that day—those big flowers were a mistake, a bad call, and belonged in her poor-judgment closet.

They sat down in the cocktail lounge. At once one of those smothering New York waiters was upon them. Clara wasted no time on him. She ordered a Campari, and as he wrote down the drinks, she said, "Bring them and then don't bother us; we have to cover lots of ground." Then she leaned toward Gina—two heads of fine hair, each with its distinct design. The girl put up her veil. "Now, Gina . . . *tell* me," said Clara.

"The ring looks wonderful on your hand. I'm glad to see it there."

No longer the au pair girl waiting to be spoken to, she held herself like a different person—equal-equal, and more. It was a great thing she had done in America.

"How did you get it into the house?"

"Where did you find it?" asked Gina.

"What does *that* mean?" Clara wanted to know. In her surprise, she fell back on the country girl's simple-minded flat tone of challenge and suspicion. "It was on my night table."

"Yes. Okay then," said Gina.

"One thing I feel terrible about is the hard assignment I gave you. Just about impossible," said Clara. "The alternative was to turn the case over to the police. I suppose you know by now that Frederic has a criminal record—no serious crimes, but they had him on Rikers Island and in the Bronx jail. That would have made trouble, an investigation would have been hard on you, and I wouldn't do that." She lowered her hand to her legs and felt the startling prominence of the muscles at the knee.

Gina did not look embarrassed by this mention of Rikers Island. She must have taken a decision not to be.

Clara never would find out what the affair with Frederic was about. Gina went no further than to acknowledge that her boyfriend had taken the ring. "He said he was walking around the apartment . . . ." Imagine, a man like that, lewd and klepto, at large in her home! "He saw the ring, so he put it in his pocket, not even thinking. I said it was given to you by someone you loved, who loved you"—so she definitely *did* understand about the love!— "and I felt responsible because it was me that brought Frederic into the house."

"That made him look blank, I suppose."

"He said that people on Park Avenue didn't understand anything. They didn't like trouble and relied on security to protect them. Once you got past the security arrangements in the lobby, why, they were just as helpless as chickens. Lucky if they weren't killed. No idea of defense."

Clara's gaze was clear and sober. Her upturned nose added dryness to her look. She said, "I have to agree. In my own place I didn't feel that I should lock away the valuables. But he may be right about Park Avenue. This is a class of people that won't think and can't admit. So it is lucky that somebody more vicious than Frederic didn't get in. Maybe Haitians are more lighthearted than some others in Harlem or the Bronx."

"Your class of Park Avenue people?"

"Yes," said Clara. She looked great-eyed again, grimly thinking, My God, what will my kids be up against! "I should thank the man for only stealing, I suppose."

"We have no time to talk about this side of it," said Gina.

These minutes in the bar seemed to be going according to Gina's deliberate plan. Frederic was not to be discussed. Suddenly Clara's impulse was to come down hard on Gina. Why, she was like the carnal woman in the Book of Proverbs who eats and drinks and wipes away all signs of lust with her napkin. But she couldn't sustain this critical impulse. Who could say how the girl got sucked in and how she managed, or what she had to do to recover the ring from such a fellow. I *owe* her. Also, with the kids she was trustworthy. Now then, what are we looking at here? There is some pride in this Gina. She stood up to the New York scene, a young upper-class Vienna girl. There *is* a certain vainglory playing through. It's false to do the carnal woman number on her. Let's not get so Old Testament. My regular Christmas card from Attica is still arriving. Before marrying this man from Daddy's bank the girl owed herself some excitement, and Gogmagogsville is the ideal place for it. Dr. Gladstone might have pointed out that Clara's thoughts were taking on a hostile color—envious of youth, perhaps. She didn't think so. Nobody, but nobody, can withstand modern temptations. (Try and print your personal currency, and see what you can get for it.) She still felt that her affection for the girl was not misplaced. "Are you sure you want to go flying back—would you think of staying?"

"What should I stay for?"

"I only wondered. If you wanted a different experience of America, you might find it in Washington, D.C."

"What would I be doing there?"

"Serious work. And don't be put off by 'serious'; it wouldn't be dull. I did some of it myself in Cortina d'Ampezzo years ago and had one of the greatest summers of my life. This friend of mine in Washington, the one I did it for, may possibly be a dark horse in the history of the American mind. I think perhaps he's the one with the gifts to put it all in perspective. Everything. If you met him, you'd agree that he was a fascinating man. . . ." Here Clara stopped herself. Without warning, she had sped into a complex intersection, a cloverleaf without a single sign. A pause was imposed on her, and she considered in a silence of many levels where her enthusiasm for this Austrian girl—a pretty girl and a sound one, basically (maybe)—was leading. Did she want to give Ithiel to her? She wanted to reward Gina. All right. And she wanted to find a suitable woman for Ithiel. It was a scandal, the wives he chose. (Or my husbands; not much better.) Again, all right. But what about Frederic? What had she done that she had to veto all discussion of the Haitian connection? And why was this conversation with

Clara cramped into twenty minutes? Why was she not invited to the farewell cocktail party? Who would be there?

Now came any number of skeptical scenarios: Gina's parents had come to America to take her home. They had paid Frederic off, and an incidental part of the deal was that he should surrender the ring. Clara could readily imagine such a package. The girl had plenty of reasons to keep Clara away from her friends—possibly her parents. Brash Clara with her hick candor might have put the case point-blank to the rich parents with all their Mitteleuropa culture (bullshit culture, Ithiel might have said). Oh, let them have their party undisturbed. But she wasn't about to send Gina to Washington all done up in gift wrapping—only the present with ribbons would have been Ithiel, handed over to this young woman. No way! Clara decided. Let me be as crude as she accused me of being. I am sure not going to make a marriage to rankle me for life. She stopped the matchmaking pitch she had begun, in her softheaded goodness. Yes, Gina was an unusual girl—that conviction was unchanged—but if Teddy Regler was the man in prospect, no.

"I haven't met him, have I?" Gina said.

"No."

Nor will you ever.

"You'd like to do something for me, wouldn't you?" Gina spoke in earnest.

"Yes, if there were something feasible," said Clara.

"You're a generous woman—exceptionally so. I'm not

in a position to go to Washington. Otherwise I might be glad to. And I have to leave you soon, I'm sorry to say. I really am sorry. There's no time to talk about it, but you have meant a lot to me."

That's one thing, Clara was thinking. The people you mean a lot to just haven't got the time to speak to you about it. "Let me tell you quickly," said Clara, "since it has to be quick, what I've been thinking of the stages a woman like me has gone through in her life. Stage one: Everybody is kindly, basically good; you treat 'em right, they'll treat you right—that's baby time. Stage two: Everybody is a brute, butcher, barbarian, rapist, crook, liar, killer and monster. Stage three: Cynicism *also* is unacceptable, and you begin to put together an improved judgment based on minimal leads or certain selected instances. I don't know what, if anything, you can make of that. . . . Now, before you leave you're going to satisfy my curiosity at least on one point: how you got the ring back. If it cost you money, I want to pay every cent of it. I insist. Tell me how much, and to whom. And how did you get into the apartment? Nobody saw you. Not with a key?"

"Don't talk about costs; there's no money owing," said Gina. "The one thing I have to tell you is how the ring got to your bedside. I went to Lucy's school and gave it to her."

"You gave an emerald to Lucy! To a young child?"

"I made sure to arrive before her new sitter came for her, and I explained to Lucy what had to be done: Here's your mother's ring, it has to be put on her night table, and here's a nice Madeira handkerchief to put it on."

"What else did you say?"

"There wasn't much else that needed saying. She knew the ring was lost. Well, it was found now. I folded the handkerchief around the ring and put it in her schoolbag."

"And she understood?"

"She's a lot like you."

"How's that? *Tell* me!"

"The same type as you. You mentioned that to me several times. Did I think so? And presently I did begin to think so."

"You could trust her to carry it out, and not to say, not to tell. Why, I was beside myself when the ring turned up on the handkerchief. Where did it drop from! Who could have done it! I even wondered if a burglar had been hired to come in and put it there. Not a word from the kid. She looked straight ahead like a Roman sentry. You asked her not to say?"

"Well, yes. It was better that way. It never occurred to you to ask her about it?"

"How would that ever come up?" said Clara. Not once. My own kid, capable of that.

"I told her to come down to the street again and report to me afterward," said Gina. "I walked behind them from school—Lucy and the new girl, who doesn't know me. And in about fifteen minutes Lucy came to me at the corner and said she had put it where I told her. . . . You're pleased, aren't you?"

"I'm mystified. I'm moved. Frankly, Gina, I don't believe you and I will ever meet again. . . ." The girl didn't disagree, and Clara said, "So I'm going to speak my mind. You weren't going to describe or discuss your experiences in New York—in Harlem: I suppose you were being firm according to your private lights. Your intimacies are your business, but the word I used to describe your attitude was 'vainglory'—the pride of a European girl in New York who gets into a mess and takes credit for getting herself out. But it's far beyond that." Tears fell from Clara's eyes as she took Gina's hand. "I see how you brought it all together through my own child. You gave her something significant to do, and she was equal to it. Most amazing to me is the fact that she didn't talk, she only watched. That level of observation and control in a girl of ten . . . how do you suppose it feels to discover that?"

Gina had been getting ready to stand up, but she briefly sat down again. She said, "I think you found the right word—right for both of us. When I came to be interviewed, the vainglory was all around—you were waving it over me. I wondered whether the lady of the house was like that in America. But you're not an American lady of the house. You have a manner, Mrs. Velde. As if you were directing traffic. 'Turn left, go right—do this, do that.' You have definite ideas."

"Pernickety, maybe?" said Clara. "Did I hurt your feelings?"

"If that means bossy, no. My feelings weren't hurt when I knew you better. You were firm, according to *your* lights. I decided that you were a complete person, and the orders you gave you gave for that reason."

"Oh, wait a minute, I don't see any complete persons. In luckier times I'm sure complete persons did exist. But now? Now that's just the problem. You look around for something to take hold of, and where is it?"

"I see it in you," said Gina. She stood up and took her purse. "You may be reluctant to believe it, because of the disappointment and confusion. Which people are the lost people? This is the hardest thing of all to decide, even about oneself. The day of the fashion show we had lunch, and you made a remark like 'Nobody is anybody.' You were just muttering, talking about your psychiatrist. But when you started to talk about the man in Washington just now, there was no nobody-anybody problem. And when the ring was stolen, it wasn't the lost property that upset you. Lost people lose 'valuables.' You only lost this particular ring." She set her finger on the stone.

How abnormal for two people, one of them young, to have such a mental conversation. Maybe life in New York had forced a girl like Gina to be mental. Clara wondered about that. "Goodbye, Gina."

"Goodbye, Mrs. Velde." Clara was rising, and Gina put her arm about her. They embraced. "With all the disorder, I can't see how you keep track. You do, though. I believe you pretty well know who you are." Gina quickly left the lounge.

Minutes ago (which might have been hours), Clara had entertained mean feelings toward the girl. She intended, even, to give her a hard time, to stroll back with her to her destination, fish for an invitation to the cocktail farewell, talk to her parents, embarrass her with her friends. That was before she understood what Gina had done, how the ring had been returned. But now, when Clara came out of the revolving door, and as soon as she had the pavement under her feet, she started to cry passionately. She hurried, crying, down Madison Avenue, not like a person who belonged there but like one of the homeless, doing grotesque things in public, one of those street people turned loose from an institution. The main source of tears came open. She found a handkerchief and held it to her face in her ringed hand, striding in an awkward hurry. She might have been treading water in New York harbor—it felt that way, more a sea than a pavement, and for all the effort and the motions that she made, she wasn't getting anywhere, she was still in the same place. When he described me to myself in Washington, I should have taken Ithiel's word for it, she was thinking. He knows what the big picture is— the big, *big* picture; he doesn't flatter, he's realistic and he's truthful. I do seem to have an idea who it is that's at the middle of me. There may not be more than one in a xillion, more's the pity, that do have. And my own child possibly one of those.

FOR THE BEST IN PAPERBACKS, LOOK FOR THE 🐧

In every corner of the world, on every subject under the sun, Penguin represents quality and variety—the very best in publishing today.

For complete information about books available from Penguin—including Pelicans, Puffins, Peregrines, and Penguin Classics—and how to order them, write to us at the appropriate address below. Please note that for copyright reasons the selection of books varies from country to country.

In the United Kingdom: For a complete list of books available from Penguin in the U.K., please write to *Dept E.P., Penguin Books Ltd, Harmondsworth, Middlesex, UB7 0DA.*

In the United States: For a complete list of books available from Penguin in the U.S., please write to *Dept BA, Penguin,* Box 999, Bergenfield, New Jersey 07621-0999.

In Canada: For a complete list of books available from Penguin in Canada, please write to *Penguin Books Canada Ltd, 2801 John Street, Markham, Ontario L3R 1B4.*

In Australia: For a complete list of books available from Penguin in Australia, please write to the *Marketing Department, Penguin Books Australia Ltd, P.O. Box 257, Ringwood, Victoria 3134.*

In New Zealand: For a complete list of books available from Penguin in New Zealand, please write to the *Marketing Department, Penguin Books (NZ) Ltd, Private Bag, Takapuna, Auckland 9.*

In India: For a complete list of books available from Penguin, please write to *Penguin Overseas Ltd, 706 Eros Apartments, 56 Nehru Place, New Delhi, 110019.*

In Holland: For a complete list of books available from Penguin in Holland, please write to *Penguin Books Nederland B.V., Postbus 195, NL–1380AD Weesp, Netherlands.*

In Germany: For a complete list of books available from Penguin, please write to *Penguin Books Ltd, Friedrichstrasse 10–12, D–6000 Frankfurt Main 1, Federal Republic of Germany.*

In Spain: For a complete list of books available from Penguin in Spain, please write to *Longman Penguin España, Calle San Nicolas 15, E–28013 Madrid, Spain.*

In Japan: For a complete list of books available from Penguin in Japan, please write to *Longman Penguin Japan Co Ltd, Yamaguchi Building, 2-12-9 Kanda Jimbocho, Chiyuoda-Ku, Tokyo 101, Japan.*